WILLOW TEMPLE

Books by Donald Hall

POETRY

Exiles and Marriages

The Dark Houses

A Roof of Tiger Lilies

The Alligator Bride

The Yellow Room

The Town of Hill

Kicking the Leaves

The Happy Man

The One Day

Old and New Poems

The Museum of Clear Ideas

The Old Life

Without

The Painted Bed

WILLOW
TEMPLE

NEW & SELECTED STORIES

Donald Hall

 Houghton Mifflin Company

BOSTON   NEW YORK   2003

For information about permission to reproduce selections from
this book, write to Permissions, Houghton Mifflin Company,
215 Park Avenue South, New York, New York 10003.

Visit our Web site: www.houghtonmifflinbooks.com.

Library of Congress Cataloging-in-Publication Data

Hall, Donald, date.
  Willow Temple : new and selected stories / Donald Hall.
    p. cm.
    Contents: From Willow Temple — The accident — The first woman —
Christmas snow — Lake Paradise — The figure of the woods — The ideal
bakery — Roast suckling pig — Widowers' woods — Argument and persuasion — The fifth box — New England primer.
    ISBN 978-0-618-44661-2
    1. United States — Social life and customs — 20th century — Fiction.
2. New England — Social life and customs — Fiction. I. Title.

PS3515.A3152 N49   2003
813'.54—dc21   2002027585

Book design by Anne Chalmers
Typeface: Linotype-Hell Fairfield

Printed in the United States of America
QUM 10 9 8 7 6 5 4 3 2 1

for Pat Barnes

Contents

Willow Temple

From Willow Temple

WE LIVED ON a farm outside Abigail, Michigan, when I was a girl in the 1930s. My father was a Latin teacher, which was how I came to be called Camilla. I cannot say that I have lived up to the name of Virgil's warrior. My father served as principal of Abigail High School, and we kept chickens and horses on our flat and scrubby land near the Ohio line. My father's schoolwork kept him busy, so we employed a succession of hired hands for chores around the farm. Many were drunks. A weekly rite, when I was small, was for my father to pay a fine on Monday morning—six A.M., before school—and drive the befuddled, thirsty, shame-faced hired man back home. When the advances for fines grew monstrous, so that our man was indentured a month ahead, he hopped a freight west. In hard times the quality of help increased, even as my father's salary and the price of eggs went down; he hired strong young men for three dollars a week, some of them sober. The poverty of those years touched everyone, even a protected child. I remember tramps coming to the back door; I remember men with gray faces whom my mother succored with milk and buttered bread. I can see one of them now, preserved among the rest because he addressed me rather than my mother. "It's hard, little girl. Could you spare a crust, little girl?"

The house was my mother's house. She was Ella, the bright face of our family, beautiful and lively—a lover of horses, poetry, and jokes. People said, lightly, that she married my father to hold herself down. I grew up loving my quiet father with a love that was equally quiet: I desperately loved my serene, passionate mother. What a beauty she was. When I see reproduced a *Saturday Evening Post* cover from the 1930s, I see my mother's face: regular features, not large but strong; bold cheekbones with good coloring; dark short hair; fullish lips deeply red without lipstick; large blue eyes, staring outward with a look both shy and flirtatious. When my mother walked into a group of strangers, the room hushed.

She had grown up with four sisters, isolated on a backcountry farm in Washtenaw County. The Great War was only a distant rumor. Her childhood was a clutch of girls, a female conspiracy on a remote, patchy forty acres, in a domain of one-room schools where half the pupils belonged to her own tribe. They made one another clothespin dolls for Christmas; they sewed and did fancywork in competition for their stepmother's praise; they passed their dreams and their dresses on to one another. How I wanted a little sister to pass my dresses and dolls on to! When my mother told me stories from her childhood, I heard themes repeated: The family was self-sufficient (I grew up reading and rereading *The Swiss Family Robinson*) and "got by on little." When she spoke of their genuine simplicity, she spoke with wonder not with bitterness; she didn't make me feel guilty over my relative comfort. The Hulze farm never prospered as the Battell's—my father's family —did for decades. The land was poor, and to survive by your own labor on your own land was triumph enough. Another theme was death, for she had lost a baby sister to a fever at eighteen months; and her mother, Patience, died of diabetes, not long before the discovery of insulin, when my mother was nine. Two years later she acquired a stepmother, my grandmother Huldah, who was kindly but fierce, with a Christianity modeled on Massachusetts Bay in the seventeenth century. Like my father, my mother was an eldest child; she mothered her younger sisters, even after Huldah's access, as Huldah quickly bore Herman Hulze two more daughters.

Life at the Hulze farm was hard—Monday washing, Tuesday ironing, Wednesday baking—but as my mother remembered it for me, it mustered grave satisfactions. Everyone worked equally, according to age and ability; everyone was clothed, warm, and well fed; in a venture of equal labor, no one depended on another's largesse. Weekdays were half school half work; the children, who rose at five *after* their parents, did housework before school, then darning or fancywork before bed. Saturday's chores finished the week and looked forward to workless Sunday. Yet Huldah's Sabbath was strenuous. Her church was two hours of hellfire in the morning, with Christian Endeavor (hymns, visiting speakers) at night. Sometimes Huldah searched out a Sunday afternoon church meeting, to occupy for her family an otherwise idle moment.

An exception to my mother's largely female nation was a dear male cousin whose story she told me when I grew older. Rudolph Howells was her first cousin, two years older, her father's sister's boy, who lived three miles down the road. Even at ages when boys and girls avoid each other, Rudy and Ella played together. They hiked to each other's houses, or barebacked a workhorse on a rare workless weekday; or they met under a great willow beside a creek halfway between them. Its shelter was their hideout, and they came to call it Willow Temple. In the absence of telephones they exchanged penny postcards to arrange their meetings. For my mother, isolated among sisters in that flat countryside, the boy's friendship was redemptive; Rudolph was the male of my mother's early life—after her father, who was alternately working or asleep. For Rudy, who was an only child, my mother provided the sole companionship close to his age. As she described him, Rudy sounds unnaturally solemn; it was Ella's childhood joy to bring out the child in Rudolph, to set him giggling or imagining extravagance. Rudy was a reader. He brought books to my mother, who became a reader herself in order to please him. In Willow Temple they recited for each other the poems they memorized at school and performed for Prize Speaking—Whittier, Longfellow, Joaquin Miller, Edgar Allan Poe, James Whitcomb Riley. My mother could say "Telling the Bees" right through, without a mistake, when she was eighty.

Rudolph was a "scholar," as Michigan country people called a serious student. In 1900 few from the farmland went to college. After the Great War people began to think about college, and to assume that Rudolph would attend the University of Michigan. As my mother late in her life told stories about Rudolph, I understood that for all his studiousness he felt some diffidence about his capacities. He worried that he would not do well at college. My mother not only made him laugh but encouraged him about his ability to leave the countryside and enroll in Ann Arbor's domestic Athens. He would *excel,* she told him. Then, doubtless, he would become a minister. What else did one go to college for?

Doctor, lawyer, teacher, pastor. Rudy in his solemnity found a way to combine the romance of his reading—the South Seas, piracy, jungles of Africa—with his dark Christianity. Some speakers at Christian Endeavor were missionaries returned from outlandish places, where they had won souls to Christ, ministering to the pigtailed hordes of China and the naked savages of the Congo. Now they traveled the Protestant Midwest to raise money for hospitals that would treat leprosy and pellagra.

When he was fourteen, Rudy left his one-room school to attend an academy in the mill town of Trieste, eleven miles away. He endured his semi-exile—boarding weekdays and coming home for weekends—until he was sixteen. For two years, my mother saw him at church every Sunday morning, and rarely at other moments except in summer. They wrote each other a midweek postcard. They remained so close that people teased them about being sweethearts, even about marrying—first cousins or not. My mother assured me that it would never have happened: They were too much brother and sister. One Sunday in the May when my mother turned fifteen, the church members packed picnics and lunched together in a field beside Goosewater Creek, not far from Willow Temple. It was Sabbath, not usually a day for picnics, but they sang hymns and listened to a Christian nurse from a mission on the island of Sapporo in Japan—a holy purpose that allowed them to eat in the fields on the Sabbath. Ella remembered Rudy at the picnic playing with a new baby, another cousin, by trundling her carriage fast and slow, making the baby Agnes jerk and laugh with abrupt stops and accelerations. After eating deviled eggs and pork sandwiches and rhubarb pie, Ella and Rudy took a long walk together, talking about their futures, and continually brushing away mosquitoes. They tramped happily among the weed trees that grew along the creek, my mother remembered, and sat inside the green dome of Willow Temple. They spoke of the university and Ella's high school, where she took Latin because Rudy had recommended it. Ella told him jokes she had saved for him. Mostly they began, "A minister, a priest, and a Christian Science practitioner . . ." One story made him laugh until he wept; she could never remember which one. When she was terribly old, and dying, Ella still recalled a small yellow butterfly abundant in the fields like migrant buttercups; she remembered the blue dress she wore, embroidered with red tulips.

That night, when Rudolph's ride came to take him back to Trieste, no one could find him. He was not in his room; he did not respond to his mother's "Yoo-hoo!" After half an hour his ride went off without him. His father and the hired man took lanterns from the barn and searched for him in the darkness among the outbuildings. Then they climbed the small pasture hill. I remember seeing that hill when I was a child. In my mind I can watch the yellow lanterns rise in the black evening, and hear the men's voices calling for him: "Rudolph! Rud-ee!" His parents were frightened; maybe Rudy had fallen taking a walk after five o'clock supper; maybe he had hit his head on a rock and lay somewhere unconscious. They summoned neighbor cousins to help.

Three miles away, asleep in bed, my mother knew nothing.

After an hour searching outside the house, the men came back, thinking to look in the rootcellar. It was Agnes's young father, cousin Michael, who found Rudolph where he had hanged himself in the attic. As Michael walked up the steep stairs with his lantern low, his face brushed against the boots. The impact pushed the boots away, and the boots swung back to hit him.

As long as any of his family lived, Rudolph's suicide was forever the subject of speculation. Rudolph — everyone repeated — was a sensible and lovable boy, affectionate if a little serious, "old for his age" but capable of playfulness. He loved his mother and father and his cousin Ella; he was a happy child. Ella's family reconstructed, by gradual accumulation of detail, the days and weeks before it happened. No one could find anything that hinted of despair or violence. Why did a bright, cheerful, beloved seventeen-year-old boy hang himself in his attic? *Why? Why? Why?* Could it have been an accident? How could he tie a noose and slip it over his head by accident? People said: It must have been something he read in a book. It was decided at the end of every discussion that reading stories caused Rudolph's death.

That Sunday night began the infection that throbbed and festered at the heart of my mother's life. Although she was warmhearted, charming, and funny, although most of her life she appeared serene or even content, I believe that a fever always burned inside her. What happened was so savage and so inexplicable that it never let her go. Over fifty and sixty and seventy years, her incredulity remained intact. She wept whenever she told me this story or made reference to it. "Oh, Camilla," she said, "why did it happen?" In my sexually obsessed youth, I tried out the notion that something had occurred or almost occurred inside Willow Temple. But my mother's continual, massive astonishment — and her absence of guilt — convinced me that nothing untoward or even unusual had happened in Willow Temple on that Sunday afternoon. For Rudolph and Ella the erotic life concealed itself under hymns and petticoats.

Part of the story was how my mother first heard the news. Monday morning, ignorant of what had happened—it was ten years before the Hulzes had a telephone—my mother took the seven o'clock train for Bosworth and its high school. Every school day of the year, she and her sister Betty took the milk train. When they sat down this morning, and the locomotive jerked forward, they heard behind them two men who had boarded three miles north, at the depot near Rudolph's house. My mother heard Mr. Peabody say to Mr. Gross what a terrible thing it was when his own father, just last night, had had to cut Rudolph Howells down from a beam in the attic. Why would a fine boy like Rudy go and kill himself?

My fifteen-year-old mother alighted at the first stop, took the next train back, and went to bed. (Betty went on to school. It was part of the story, always, that Betty continued to school.) Ella vomited and for three days would not eat. She stayed home the rest of the school year, four weeks. She turned pale, lost weight; Dr. Fowles said that she was anemic. Once a week a Trieste butcher sent two quarts of steer's blood for Huldah to store in the icebox. My mother drank a tumbler of blood every day; it nauseated her, but mostly she kept it down. Once she left her bed and slipped from the house for half a day—terrifying her father and Huldah—to walk by the creek until she came to Willow Temple, where she crept inside and howled hysterical tears. ("I thought he would be there," she told me when she was old. *"Camilla, I thought he was there."*) Thereafter her family contrived to keep her in bed. She failed all summer, eating little, until one evening she heard Huldah's harsh voice in the garden beyond her window, telling a visitor, "We're going to lose our big girl."

This overhearing or eavesdropping appeared to startle my mother back to life. By the time school opened in September she had become bright and energetic again—brighter and more energetic than before. After her mourning, she turned from a shy fifteen-year-old into the creature who caused the intake of breath. As her beauty became obvious for the first time, her youthful life began. She took part in high school literary and theatrical groups, as much as commuting allowed her. A year later, in her senior year, she boarded in Bosworth weekdays. If a hayride or a square dance took place on a Saturday night, she stayed over in town for the weekend, despite Huldah's disapproval. The summer after graduation, turned seventeen, she took a job at Gotwig's department store in Ann Arbor, staying with a family related to her own mother.

It was clear, when my mother recollected, that Ann Arbor raised a pleasant devil in her. When another boarder arranged a blind date for her with a university student, she undertook a new life, and its excitement still reverberated when she was eighty and remembered those years. She became *popular*, a powerful word in the vocabulary of the time, and dated many young men. One fraternity—my father never belonged to one; it would have been unthinkable—elected Ella Hulze its sweetheart, granting her an honor normally reserved for a sorority girl. She would have joined a sorority if she had been a student. (When I attended the university, I joined one and quit after six months.) My mother dated almost every night, she told me, and her engagement book was full a month ahead. She made me laugh with her stories of boys she dated—a collateral Ford who drove a Stutz; a broker-to-be who waxed his red mustache into points; a fainting swain who sent long-stemmed roses to Gotwig's.

"It was innocent," she told me when I was seventeen. Ten years later I reminded her of that word, when she stayed with me after my daughter's birth. She laughed and said, "It was *mostly* innocent, Camilla." She told me about driving to Chicago in a roadster for a weekend with two fraternity boys. They visited a speakeasy, after she took a room at the YWCA. She had to ring a bell to be let in at three A.M., and she covered her mouth to disguise her breath. She returned to Ann Arbor on Monday at seven A.M. to drink coffee and attend her counter at Gotwig's. A week later, both boys died at dawn in the same roadster, careering off the road into a maple tree near Walled Lake after a night of Prohibition gin and jazz. When she met my father, as he shopped for his family's Christmas, my mother was ready to settle down. They were engaged by Easter. My mother was eighteen then, my father twenty-six.

She clerked in a department store; he was a graduate student in classical languages. People speak of the attraction of opposites. Opposites are attracted when each is anxious about its own character. (And I am their product, in old age still a woman anxious about the conflicts in her character.) I think of my father as he must have appeared in 1925: He came from country people as she did, but he wore eyeglasses and lived for books—not only books, but books in an ancient language. My mother had taken Latin for two years of high school, but she stopped after Rudy died. How did my father find the courage to approach the beautiful Ella Hulze? I suppose his innocence was his courage; eight years older, bound to his library carrel, he would not have known that she was *popular*. Billy, or William, had reached a moment in his life, halfway through a last year of study, with a high school teaching job waiting for him, when he was ready for courtship and marriage. Through a recent legacy from a godmother, who had married into Flint's auto industry, he had fifteen hundred dollars, which would provide the down payment on a house at a mortgage of two and a half percent. Possibly his studies contributed to his infatuation: I laughed when I learned, not long before he died, that in his final seminar at Michigan he had examined Ovid's *Art of Love*. Like Ella, my father jolted himself into looking for an opposite. Then he met a beautiful girl, from a Michigan farm, selling scarves at Gotwig's.

Maybe William was not quite so opposite as he appeared to be. After all, he grew up outside Abigail on a hog farm—prosperous for many decades—that his parents and bachelor brother worked until foreclosure in 1937. Billy became the Latinist— "William Hammersmith Battell," as his diplomas read, and "foremost scholar in the history of Abigail High," as the *Abigail Journal* called him—who majored in classics at the University of Michigan. He was first in his family to finish high school, much less college. After he made Phi Beta Kappa in 1922, he returned to raise pigs with his father and his brother. He did this on principle, full of Roman republican notions; he enjoyed tales of colonial American blacksmiths who read forty lines of Hebrew before dawn. A pig farmer who translated Latin poetry seemed no anomaly to my father.

But my father was not a skillful farmer. When pig raising did not take his full attention, he felt inadequate or hypocritical; in his absent-mindedness, he failed his agrarian ideals. The Latin language, and only the Latin language, enthralled him. Exhausted after a day among hogs, he sat by the oil lamp that rose from a central table in the small living room, reading Tacitus while his mother darned and his brother studied baseball scores and his father snored into sleep. In Virgil's *Georgics*, the Michigan farm crossed paths with the study of Latin. As a young man my father dreamed of translating the *Georgics*, adapting them to southern Michigan, but the farming tired him out; he never completed the first book.

By 1925 it was obvious that the Battell farm could not support four adults. The agricultural depression had started a decade before the rest of the country crashed, and the once rich farm began to fail. Somebody had to leave the place and get a job. Then came the disaster, as my father always called it. One of his chores was to feed the piglets after they were weaned from their great mothers, carrying buckets of corn from the Battell cribs. The stored feed nourished a guerrilla army of rats. One morning my young father, weary after staying up with Virgil half the night, fed rat poison to sixty-seven young pigs. The whole family wept, even his hard father and stolid brother, as they dug a long trench on a rainy day and buried their hopes for a prosperous or even a tolerable year. When he was an old man he shook his head in melancholy guilt as he spoke of his lethal error. "The bags were different colors and sizes. The pellets were gray. How could I have done it?" I remember him at seventy-four, still lamenting his terrible mistake; he could see the pale young bodies in the rain, and puddles gathering in the trench. My mother, the family wit and teaser, knew better than to joke about the disaster. But once, when my father was soaring high in self-confident distraction — and made tea by pouring hot coffee over tea leaves — she called him "the Great Poisoner." He laughed, I remember, but looked abashed and sorrowful.

After the disaster the Battell family took out a mortgage to provide capital for my father's M.A. at the university. Back in Ann Arbor, my father undertook courses in education as well as Greek and Latin, so that he might become a high school teacher. He had returned to his studies for two months when he met my mother in Gotwig's. The elderly Miss Wuestefeld of Abigail High, who had taught Billy, had told him that she would hold on until William was finished with graduate school. Thus my father revisited, ten years afterward, the classroom where he had learned to chant *amo amas amat*, and eagerly led new students to recite *amo amas amat*. It was a secure position, as everyone knew: "There'll always be work for a Latin teacher." A monthly check would repay his family's bank loan, and help to repair his conscience that mourned the poisoned piglets. In Abigail, his old schoolmates would breed him pupils and call him "professor" without irony. My parents had been married three years and I was a baby when the position of principal opened. It was not his administrative ability that recommended my father. Most teachers were women but principals were men; only men could deal with unruly boys. Maybe my mother was unruly too.

My early life was happy — or at least it was *even*, like a plain steadily upthrusting a crop of corn. The radio and the automobile were our wonders, and I measure my childhood by the names of products: the Crosley, the Emerson, the Philco; the Model T, the brief blue Chevrolet, the Model A that never broke down as we took rides every Sunday afternoon in good weather, adventurously speeding at forty miles an hour over Michigan backcountry roads, knowing where we were headed without being sure how we would get there. My parents sat together in the front seat and I sat in the back, scooting from side to side in my Sunday dress as the landscape drew me. Having access to both sides was a luxury of my only-child-hood. On these drives my parents spoke little. I watched my father's mild bespectacled eyes take in an Angus herd; I gazed at my mother's poised, beautiful profile as her face turned left and right, calm or complacent, accepting what the route offered. Every Sunday we rode two or three hours over southern Michigan and northern Ohio, looking at cattle, chickens, turkeys, pigs, and horses. When we had driven as far as we would go, and started back, my father would search out an ice cream parlor and treat us to a sundae.

Always we returned in order to ride our horses for an hour before Sunday night supper, which was sandwiches around the radio. I cannot remember when Jack Benny's show began broadcasting, but in my old age Jack Benny's running gags, remembered, taste of cream cheese and crushed pineapple. My mother and I rode together after school in good weather. On Saturdays as well as Sundays all three of us saddled up: my father's horse, the roan stallion Bigboy, unruly like a high school boy, my mother's Morgan mare Benita, and my multicolored pony Skylark, who was large enough to carry my slight figure until I was sixteen. These handsome creatures were the enduring quotidian romance of my girlhood. After school I curried Skylark's flanks before my mother was ready for our amble along a stony road at the side of a hayfield. Both my parents grew up with workhorses, and would have missed equine company had we not stabled them in the barn adjacent to our chickens. I'm not sure why we kept chickens, except that my father considered farming *a good thing*—and he no longer cared to raise pigs. Selling eggs and broilers paid for the hired men and the horses.

When my mother sat a horse she looked not like a Michigan farmgirl but like the Honorable Lady Something; she wore a horse the way a model wears clothes. My father was unpredictably impetuous, an excellent rider on a capricious powerful horse. Bigboy liked to run, and would have run away if my father had not been so masterful; they galloped ahead of us and galloped back, pulling up in a froth of high spirits. One of my mother's teasing names for my father was Billy Cowboy.

In my earliest recollections my parents acted like lovers, if not quite like a pastoral shepherd and shepherdess. Although they were polite in the old-fashioned way, they took every opportunity to touch each other. When they didn't want me to understand something, they talked Latin, or something Latinish enough to confuse me. My father delighted, in his mild fussy way, in their domestic classicism. *Equus* was an early word, not to mention *amor*. Before I was seven I knew that *via* meant road and that we would take a ride in the Model A. Horses were every day and the Model A was Sundays. I cherished those afternoons in the back seat. I cherish them still, as I approach my seventies. In my life, when I have been especially troubled—my daughter died in childhood; I divorced my husband—I have found myself for comfort playing back mental films of those afternoons in the back seat of a Ford exploring the flat country roads.

Driving the car, my father, I imagine, daydreamed Latin. I

have no notion what my mother dreamed. Maybe she thought of my father, or of Rudolph. Because Rudolph was the source of my mother's Latin, and because he and my father were both serious or even solemn, I came to think of Rudolph as an antecedent to my father. I considered that my mother made up for losing Rudolph when she married William. I was shy to advance this theory to my mother until she was well into her eighties. "Perhaps," she said, but it was clear that my notion annoyed her. "They did not look alike at all," she said, and a moment later wiped her eyes.

My mother learned to drive — a fairly advanced notion for a small-town housewife in 1933 — in order to go to the library, so that she and I could stock up on books. I progressed from dog-and-cat books to a good anthology of poems called *Silver Pennies*. Next I found novels, from *Rebecca of Sunnybrook Farm* to *Black Beauty*, with excursions into the Nancy Drew series, and started to inhabit the house of stories, in love with the improbable and the heroic. My mother enjoyed novels and biographies but cared more for poetry: She deserted Whittier for Wordsworth and Longfellow for Keats, but she also admired the moderns: Sara Teasdale, Edna St. Vincent Millay, John Masefield, Elinor Wylie, Edwin Arlington Robinson. She wore out a copy of *Tristram*. Later she found Robert Frost — my father admired Frost, the classical side — and the young Stephen Vincent Benét. It would have been too much for her to admire T. S. Eliot or Wallace Stevens; later, when I tried them on her — I was at college — she shook her head regretfully.

My father reread Virgil, Horace, and Catullus; he preferred Cicero's letters to his orations; he worked away at Thucydides with his slimmer Greek, read journals of classical studies—and increasingly took part in a battle over the place of Latin studies in the American high school curriculum. Voices in the 1930s proclaimed that learning Latin was impractical, that our youth should not waste valuable time on dead languages, should concentrate on arithmetic, mechanical drawing, and business letters. To my father, the suggestion was retrograde. In Abigail he tried to institute at least one year of Latin for all students, with four years for those few aiming toward college. Two years of Latin, with a B average, were required for admission to the University of Michigan.

He gave speeches after lunch at the Rotary Club; he wrote letters to the *Abigail Journal*. Although principal he still taught Latin, and because he taught with enthusiasm, Abigail's Latin courses were well subscribed. Elsewhere the walls were falling. When an old Detroit high school chose to remove "Classical Academy" from its name, he wrote a letter to the *Detroit News*, ending, "If our civilization is to survive encroaching darkness, Latin and Greek must keep alight the fires of learning, shining beacons that keep us to the path." He signed it "William Hammersmith Battell, Principal, Abigail High School." If I let him sound pompous, remember that he pursued a passion.

With his duties as chairman of the Michigan Classical Association, and as secretary of the Great Lakes Latin Society, he paid less attention to our farm, haphazardly preserved by the succession of hired men. The first I remember is Herbert Ganke, an old man who talked to himself while he worked. He was courtly to me and my mother; he worked slowly but steadily. Once a month he got into trouble: Finally he passed out in a widow's back yard after stealing clothes from her clothesline. There were also boys who worked a week or two and vanished; a sweet hobo named Tom lasted a whole winter, sleeping under the eaves in the hired man's room. He disappeared after payday when the snowdrops poked up. A shy, handsome local boy named Raymond was expert with horses, and could even control the volatile Bigboy. Raymond was illiterate, my mother discovered, and she taught him to read. There were men named Merton, Douglas, Miller, and Ferdinand.

Late afternoons, when my father came home from school, and my mother and I were back from our ride, he changed into overalls, consulted with the latest hand, and checked out the hens while my mother assembled supper. I attended our one-room school a quarter of a mile away, and sometimes brought a friend, Caroline or Rebecca, back to play; but on rainy days or when I played alone with my dollhouse or read stories, I interrupted myself to visit the barn and the outbuildings with Miller or Raymond or Herbert, currying Skylark, feeding apples to Skylark, Benita, and (carefully) Bigboy. Some hands were grumpy, possibly not fond of small girls, as I followed them around; others took the opportunity to smoke cigarettes and tell the stories of their lives. There was always a fourth setting at table—often an intriguing presence for a child. With Raymond I was in love; after school I liked it when Raymond sat at the kitchen table doing his ABCs under my mother's supervision, reading my cat-and-dog books from the attic, moving on to *Silver Pennies*.

When I was eight or nine, my father's advocacy of classical studies became my father's unrelenting obsession. In memory, his passion seems to have occupied most of my childhood; in reality, it probably took two years. Every night my father read bulletins from the Department of Education, or a mimeographed sheet from the university's classics department, or *The American Classicist.* Every day the mail brought letters, bulletins, and notices. William Hammersmith Battell founded the Southeastern Michigan Secondary School Classical Studies Association. When he came home from school to desk, he studied not Horace but statistics about classroom study of Horace's language. My father ignored my mother and me in order to defend Cicero in the senate of popular opinion. My mother and I still took our afternoon rides on Skylark and Benita, sometimes with Raymond on Bigboy, who needed the exercise, but no longer did the family go on Sunday afternoon joyrides in the Model A. Sometimes my father brought me with him, on a Saturday afternoon in the car, to visit someone engaged in the same struggle; they had long, intense conversations while I tried talking with strange children or knitting mittens or reading my book. My mother stayed home. She read her poets; she kept up with darning and the prodigious canning of summer. She again took up quilting, which she had learned as a girl, to occupy her hours while my father spent himself elsewhere. He approved of quilting, classic if not Latin, but his enthusiasm was principled. Ella lacked theoretical passions. When my mother's spectacular patchwork took a red ribbon at the Michigan State Fair in 1937, it was clear that the Idea of Quilthood—not this extravagant bright assemblage—exalted my father's reasonable soul. "*Splendidissimus,*" he said.

Often my mother and I remained alone together on weekends, quiet in the living room, or riding over dusty fields, while my father drove overnight to Mackinaw Island to chair an emergency meeting called by Michigan Concerned Latinists. No longer did my parents touch each other when they passed in the hallway. My father behind rimless glasses gazed into the distance, airy with urgency. My mother's beautiful eyes looked low at hooked rugs and waxed floors, and I heard her sighing, sighing, sighing. I knew she was unhappy and I sighed as I heard her sigh.

For my tenth birthday, in March of 1938, my parents gave me the sheepdog I had begged for. Memory of Dido as a puppy allows me to date events of that spring, because I recollect her with a love purer than any other; Skylark was dear but did not follow me to school and to bed. At the library I discovered Albert Payson Terhune's *Lad: A Dog* and its siblings. With my mother I trained Dido; I slept with her; I grew up with her—and when she died of old age at the farm (I was in graduate school, in a female co-op that forbade animals), I died with her. She was ancient, and my mourning was extravagant. When she died I lost my memory of tranquillity in early childhood—a peace that had shattered, as it happened, not long after Dido's arrival. I suppose that Dido's death was my second—as my mother died first with Rudolph, then in a roadster's wreckage. The spring of Dido, I endured a disaster of distrust while I hugged my trembling, ecstatic dog.

A month or two after my birthday I woke to hear my parents quarreling. I slept lightly that spring, as Dido wriggled under the covers or signaled that she needed to go out. It wasn't an argument that I heard first; it was the sound of my father crying unmitigated tears—a sound I had never before heard. He was not an unemotional man, as men went in those days, and I had heard him weep over a friend's death; but that night I heard a terrible sound—my father's wail of utter misery, as he gagged and coughed and spluttered. My heart pounded and I left my bed in order to run to their room, but then my mother's soft continual murmur — controlled, persistent — held me back and calmed me, as it was intended to calm my father. I had no notion of the matter of his tears. I heard no words from him except "Ella" among the cries, and "Ella" repeated. When I made out her words, I heard her say that she loved him — but the words carried a cadence of withholding, like "anyway" or "still" or "despite everything." She was trying to console him, but in her tone I heard something I had never heard before, as chilly as a wheatfield in January.

For some nights — a week? a month? — I stayed awake deliberately in order to listen. I could not hear everything they said, and maybe I slept through a night or two, though I doubt it. I heard enough. With Dido's wriggling help, I conspired to hear my new parents, my parents as I had never known them. After years of our daily routine — farm, school, horses, chickens, canning, quilting, Sunday rides, radio, Virgil — I entered a moonless darkness of conspiracy as frigid as the stars. Everywhere I went, I carried with me this enormous debilitating secret, something I could not speak of to anyone — not to Rebecca in the hayloft, not to my teacher at school, not to my cousins.

Night after night, when they thought I was asleep, I heard them quarrel. Sometimes they attacked each other. My mother's voice rose and I heard her use the word "divorce," a notion I scarcely understood. I heard my father say, "I'll take the child," and I realized the identity of the creature. Increasingly now they mentioned "him," and I became aware that my mother loved someone other than my father. I hugged Dido so hard that she made a squeaking noise, then licked my face. Lying in bed with my dog, my heart pounding, I knew whom my mother loved. Only a short time before, just after my birthday, I had come home from school to find my mother agitated, not looking at me, running back and forth to tidy or do small chores. She told me that Raymond no longer worked for us — the boy she taught to read — and that old Ferdinand was back, to fill in for a while. I never liked Ferdinand, who ignored a child, and I adored Raymond, so I burst into tears. My mother turned on me in a rage (something she never did, not even when I broke a cup of wedding china) and shouted, "Go to your room!"

It was Raymond whom my mother loved instead of my father. That Raymond was ten years younger than she was — feckless though sweet, illiterate, diffident, from a family that lived in a shack, with a father often in jail — did not then occur to me. Later I put things in their places: My father had raised himself up, become learned, dedicated himself to the finer things, became "professor" in Abigail; how it must have pummeled him, along with profounder jealousy, that my mother picked Raymond to love — Raymond who had never graduated from grammar school. Doubtless my mother loved Raymond at least partly because he was so pitiable, so unlike my distinguished father. Something about Raymond was pathetic or beaten, something hangdog. The combination of prettiness and need made him so attractive.

Listening to my stranger-parents, in their hurts and deliberations, I felt terror and misery. But also I felt exalted: I was a romantic figure, like a child in a book, like the match girl in the snow, wistful pathetic product of adult abandonment or deceit.

In my conspiracy or secret knowledge, in my separation from my parents and the rest of my world—friends and school and house, everyone but Dido, who listened to my complaints ecstatic with adoration—I felt myself the locus of an extraordinary fate. I thrilled myself by the vision of my despair. I felt ennobled by self-pity and by awareness of, and admiration for, my mother's recklessness, beauty, abandon, and sin.

One night I heard my father say, "Damn you to hell!"—he never swore—and laugh when my mother took offense. It was as if I had been stolen by gypsies. It was as if they had been gypsies always, disguising themselves as ordinary Michigan people. During the day—I was sleepy of course; my mother puzzled when I dozed in my school dress on the hearth rug after school—my parents tried to carry on as they had always done. I was impressed by the aplomb with which they behaved "for the child's sake." Their ability to deceive, to be utterly different by day and by night, carved itself into my soul. My father came home from school, put on his overalls, did a few chores with Ferdinand, spoke politely with my mother over dinner, and asked Camilla about her schoolwork. We performed a conspiracy of three, a play for three voices. I pretended or dissembled as much as they did, and rejoiced in the skill of my deceit. I pretended ignorance or innocence, as I knew for certain that my parents were cruel enemies inside the appearance of their marriage. Although they continued as if they cared for me, I was an alien encumbrance. We were three strangers, as only I was aware.

Officially I did not know the facts of life, as we called sex in those years, because parents waited to tell a daughter until she was ready to menstruate. But as a farm child I had watched barnyard copulation. Already I attempted to read novels written for adults in which men and women—when they loved each other, whether they were married or not—disappeared into the privacy of a blank page to do something which confirmed their love and made for mayhem. I knew that what they did was wicked and wonderful, the most extreme of pleasures and the worst. I knew that my mother and Raymond—while my father and I were at school, or on weekends when my father and I visited someone— did what the rooster did with the hens, what the stallion Bigboy attempted with the neutered mare Benita.

One night as my parents spoke in bed, I understood that they approached a crisis. The next night at nine o'clock Raymond would come to the house and the three of them would talk. From what was said, I gathered that they would decide about divorce and about "the child." The next night after dinner my father proposed that we ride in the car. It was unheard of, that I stay up after seven on a school night; they wanted to tire me out so that I would sleep soundly. Disingenuously I remarked on my late bedtime, and in a single voice my parents said that it didn't matter, that I could sleep in and be late for school. They seemed unaware how unprecedented their behavior was.

That night I did not need to struggle to stay awake; I set my bedroom door ajar and crouched on the floor with my ear at the opening, hugging Dido, so that I would miss nothing. I heard Raymond—he had an unusual gait—walk up the path. I heard him enter; I heard perfunctory conventional exchanges. How frightened Raymond must have been. I could imagine his drawn, white, lean, weak, handsome face. I heard my father's level voice, grave and formal; I heard my mother weeping; I heard a new sound which I could identify as Raymond's tears. Later, I heard my father weeping also—three grownups crying in the living room at the foot of the long stairs.

Maybe I dropped off to sleep, leaning between the doorjamb and Dido, for the next sound I heard was a shout of rage or despair, then hurried steps and the door slamming and steps running outside. Raymond had run away. I pushed my face around the jamb of the door and saw that my father and my mother stood side by side. Suddenly I heard my father scream, "Bitch!" The front door hurtled open again, my father shouted, "I'll never be back!"—and the door slammed again. I crept to the top of the stairs. My mother stood in the doorway as the Model A started and my father drove away. When she turned back and entered the living room, I stood halfway down the stairs in my white nightgown, a fierce Virgilian warrior who had read Victorian romances. "I have known all," I said.

Within two months, my father quit all his associations and societies. In a year his subscriptions ran themselves out. He dismissed Ferdinand, came home earlier from school, and did long weekend chores, farming without help. Later, he canceled his annual order for three hundred chicks and let his poultry venture dwindle to eggs for our household. He traded Bigboy for an older, more tractable gelding called Rusty, and we three rode together again.

The night of the confrontation, my father could not have stayed away for long. We ate breakfast together the next morning. I remember because we had pancakes, a rarity usually saved for birthdays. In my ten-year-old cynicism, I made note of our treat.

My mother could not look me in the eye; my father praised the pancakes and left quickly, but behaved toward me with his competent affectation of ordinariness, which let me understand that my mother had not spoken of my eavesdropping.

When she saw me on the stairs, as she turned back from the door, her face went dead white. After I made my rehearsed announcement, she struggled to recover herself and asked questions to find out what I knew. At once I dissembled; her aspect terrified me, and in order to bring blood back into her face, I lied or played innocent. When she asked me what I had known, I answered only by saying that my father was not coming back. My mother assured me, grasping for an appearance of calm, that he didn't mean it. Forcing a frail smile, she said, "He'll be back soon, Camilla." They had quarreled about the horses; she wanted him to sell Bigboy . . . When I kept my silence then, my secrecy resumed itself forever. My secrecy dug itself a lightless castle inside the hill. My secrecy bricked up a dungeon door behind which something still languishes.

Our lives restored themselves; at least theirs did or seemed to. I doubt that my mother saw Raymond again. Four or five years later, he was killed in the war; I know that much only because his name with its gold star ornaments the scroll by the Abigail Town Hall. If anyone else came into my mother's life, later or earlier, I never knew it. My father went back to his Latin classes and his school administration. Every day after chores he sat down to his books, Lucretius more than Virgil, Tacitus more than Livy, some Horace but never Ovid. In the evenings he studied while my mother quilted or revisited her poets, or read novels aloud to my father and me: Dickens, Mark Twain, early Steinbeck. After a while they were touching each other again. I watched with careful, secretive eyes. Two years later my mother had a hysterectomy and told me I would remain an only child.

Surely I was changed forever. Life at the farm was calm, but I lived elsewhere in my fancy. I absented myself reading stories, imagining myself a reckless heroine and a pathetic victim. Outside the house of fiction I was chronically restless. Nothing in life, I knew, was what it appeared to be. When I read a story by Nathaniel Hawthorne, I recognized the minister and his pious congregation who met at midnight in the woods to celebrate Mass for the devil. I knew that by universal conspiracy we agreed to deny the wickedness of every human being. We needed, every hour, to understand: The fabric of routine covered unseen deceptions and enormities. We also needed to remember that the cloth must show no rips or tears, and this covering was as real as anything. I admired the fabrics my father and my mother wove, whatever might throb or coil underneath the cloth.

When I left home at eighteen to attend the University of Michigan, I contrived to continue the life of fiction. I delighted in keeping two or three boyfriends at the same time; my schemes provided opportunity for plot-making. Majoring in English I found Henry James, and wrote an honors thesis on *What Maisie Knew*—and I knew what Maisie knew better than my teachers did. My parents were pleased with my academic success. My father offered to finance a Ph.D. if I wished to enter his profession as a college teacher, but I wanted to write rather than to talk about the writing of others. I won a Hopwood in fiction, took an M.A. in library science, and spent many years working in the library of Barnaby Academy in Grosse Arbor, a boys' boarding school outside Detroit. I was a servant in the house of fiction, and in the houses of history, poetry, and biography. I found it less necessary to dissemble, in my private life, as I plotted and published my own literary fictions. Critics sometimes wondered at the violence in my stories, not aware of my provenance as a warrior.

My history is not especially interesting; nor was my parents' history, so far as I can tell, after the incident of Raymond. They lived the even life of the cornfields, with their horses and Chevrolets, with their quilts and classical studies. I visited sometimes for weekends. Sometimes we met in Detroit or Ann Arbor for a play or a concert. When I married they approved of my husband, and when Valerie was born my mother spent two weeks sleeping on the sofa to help me out. We lived in a dormitory then, for my husband taught French at the Academy, and my mother's aging beauty did not escape the attention of the sixteen-year-olds in our hall. During the long illness of my daughter—she contracted leukemia at five, when medicine seldom cured leukemic children —my parents tendered comfort and support. They took a new mortgage after paying off their old, to help with expenses; more importantly, they supplied their presence, their grief, and their abundant tears.

Our marriage could not survive Valerie's death. My husband and I could scarcely look at each other, and both of us found comfort elsewhere. I fell in love with a student, as it happens, and caused considerable suffering. When my ex-husband, Emil, suddenly flew off to teach at the American School in Beirut, the football coach's ex-wife went with him. This elopement led to Emil's subsequent fame, if that's the word: three and a half years as a hostage; freedom; talk shows; a book, in which "an early marriage" received mention.

For two decades I remained in the Barnaby library; the school authorities never acknowledged my escapade—if they ever knew. I settled down among the books and the boys who read books. My fiction enjoyed some success, so the English department borrowed me to teach a writing class. When I was forty-five I married a widower retired from Chrysler, a rare executive who loved theater and literature, and we led a good life together until he died, nine years later. I found relative comfort in middle age, as I suppose my parents did.

But I need to say: Even through the worst times—torments and disasters, losses, gains that were worse than losses—I kept on loving my parents. Whatever they did in the dark of the moon, they performed as well as they could in daylight. I honored their brave, sad endeavor. When I sought calm, waiting for electroshock during depression in the worst years, I thought again of Sunday rides in the Model A—seeing the back of my mother's neck, and my father's trim haircut.

When Latin went down to defeat after the war, my father withdrew from teaching but remained principal of Abigail High until he retired at sixty-five, subject of farewell banquets and testimonials. He lived for eleven more years, pruning fruit trees and raising berries on the farm he had brought his bride to. Occasionally he worked at translating Lucretius into blank verse, a project with which my mother helped; her ear for iambic pentameter was more assured than my father's. I keep the unfinished manuscript with its fussy Victorian diction. When he died, my mother remained on the old place; I moved here when she was eighty, five years after my second husband died. I read *Tristram* aloud to her, along with *Rabbit, Run.* We walked every day in the pine woods that grew where hayfields had been. We drove to Ann Arbor for the bookstores and visited Gotwig's, which appeared to have shrunk. We drove to Detroit to see the Rivera murals again. In desultory fashion, I finished a quilt she had started, and I held my mother's hand when she died last year at eighty-seven. I board my horse at a neighbor's farm; my latest collie is another Dido; I live in the house where everything happened.

Or almost everything. In her last years my mother kept returning in her mind to her cousin Rudolph, and told me much of what I recounted earlier. I listened hard to understand her, Ella still beautiful in the noble bones of her lean ninth-decade face. When I heard her speak of Rudy's young pedantry, expressed in bookishness and missionary Christianity, I thought of my father, although my father was never troubled by diffidence. Then I made the association that annoyed her. Once as she spoke of Rudy she revealed something else, or two things at once: Rudolph's eyes, she said, were a blue-gray that you never forgot — light and mild yet so piercing they were painful to look at. She remembered such eyes in one other face only, a farmhand's named Raymond, she said, whom I had probably forgotten.

Her mind remained sharp, although she sometimes wandered among episodes of the past. "Nothing happened," she told me during the last month of her life, "in Willow Temple that day." I knew what day she meant. "But maybe he felt something," she said, and stopped speaking.

"Maybe he wanted something to happen?" I said.

"I've thought so," she said. "Maybe he felt something in his trousers. I've wondered so." I held her hand. "It could have been something as small as that." Then her old humor asserted itself: "Not that I had witnessed his dimensions!" She laughed her trim laugh. "It was so long ago," she said. "He wanted so much to go to China. What if something *had* happened in Willow Temple? Sometimes I think he never died." She shook her head to deny dementia. "Sometimes I think he never lived—or that I never lived, or your father. How preposterous we are. Jokes and disasters, that's all there are. Is." Her tone suggested that she spoke without consequence. "The world is arbitrary," she went on. "Why did I work at Gotwig's? Why did the pigs die? Why do poets write poems? If insulin had been discovered, I would never have known Huldah; I might have been a Christian. Why did Raymond put a noose around his head?"

Some mistakes you don't point out. Some mistakes lack great implication, though I suspect that nothing is wholly arbitrary, not mistaken names nor poisoned pigs nor leukemia nor a kidnapping in Beirut. The latest Dido let me understand that she wanted to go outside, and I took her walking past fallen outbuildings into the new wood.

THE ACCIDENT

TOWARD THE END of the war, when David Bardo was fourteen
and fifteen, his mother and father took him to dinner at the
Bunkerville Tavern twice a week. It was the family indulgence.
Tuesdays and Thursdays David's father drove from his office in
Green City to the electric company's Bunkerville branch. On
those afternoons David's mother walked to meet David outside
Grover Country Day at three-thirty and they took a bus six miles
north to the tavern. Taking the bus saved a cupful of Esso and a
few miles on the old Pontiac's tires; tires and gas were hard to
come by in those years. After dinner at the tavern Mr. Bardo
drove carefully home to Green City's suburb of Grover.

David's parents drank Scotch before dinner at the Bunkerville Tavern. David and his mother arrived at four, walked a
block from the bus stop, and joined his father, who sat with
Stewie Brewster and Ham Heinz, both of whom worked at the
electric company. Stewie and Ham spent much of their time in
the warmth of the dark tavern, slouched in mahogany-stained
booths with red plush cushions, under small-wattage lights in
wall brackets, with a waiter named Goose who brought drinks
from a long mahogany bar tended by Bobbo.

Welcome was warm, Black & White copious, and the hours

lapsed like snow falling. The tavern was a shadowy smoky gregarious retreat attached to a large bright restaurant with a dance floor and an orchestra on Friday and Saturday nights. David and his parents mostly stayed away from the crowded weekends. Ham and Stewie were always there, but on weekends Bobbo was too busy to join them, as he often did Tuesdays and Thursdays.

As David sat in the booth, he watched degrees of tipsiness grow and alter. When his mother felt woozy, she made a quick trip to the bathroom and stuck her finger down her throat to clear her head, then returned to a fresh Scotch. One night she came back from the ladies' to one of Ham's monologues on modern art. "I don't know what this Picasso gets away with it." *Life* had just run a feature. "My kids," said Ham, shaking his head repeatedly.

To David's surprise, his mother took up the subject of painting, addressing Stewie, not Ham, as Ham continued to grumble in the direction of David and his father. With one ear David heard his mother saying that she longed to paint watercolors. There were places in South Carolina that she remembered from her girlhood, that she could see right now as pretty as that calendar, that she had always wanted to paint. Stewie nodded frequently, his mother repeated herself, and David had an idea. A month later, on his mother's birthday, David gave her a wooden box of watercolor paints and brushes with an instruction book and a pad of paper. When he reminded her that she wanted to paint scenes recollected from girlhood, she expressed enthusiasm, but after a week the wooden box went into a closet.

At the Bunkerville Tavern David lived at the edge of an adult society, drinking multiple Cokes and listening to talk that loosened and became more giddy as the rounds mounted. Kidding was the local language, running gags and references to the foibles of absent friends. "Joe is just an accident waiting to happen." Everybody laughed. At seven o'clock they ordered dinner. His parents ate fish for the war effort, and David ordered meatloaf with mushroom sauce; it was mostly bread, his mother reassured him. Ham seldom ate, or allowed his turkey tetrazzini to turn cold in front of him while he smoked and drank. Stewie regularly ordered a strip steak, not on the menu, and hinted that Mr. Mazzola, shadowy owner of the tavern, had arrangements with a butcher who had his own arrangements. "Hey, Goose," Stewie said one night, pushing his plate away after one bite, "this thing is terrible. This thing is horse."

Goose liked to make them laugh. "No, sir," he said, tossing his head to indicate levity. "It's Jap mule. The cook thought he'd try it out. Just a minute, I'll get you your usual steak, Mr. Brewster."

"Little yellow bastards," said Ham dreamily.

"Long as it's not Jap soldier," said Stewie.

It was pleasant enough for David to reside on a fringe of adulthood, listening to the false, consistent, drunken world of the grownups. An only child, he felt strange with other children, most of whom had brothers or sisters. Here, he was allowed to remain separate, and David enjoyed his privileged exile. He was not party to the adult wisecracks and repetitions, which played the same melody over and over. He was allowed to be alien, as he had always felt that he was. When he was younger, his parents had often invited three couples to the house to play bridge, while David lay upstairs in his room. There were drinks with bridge, and David used to listen as the voices grew louder and the laughter more raucous. From his bed, David heard not words or sentences but the tones and rhythms of speech. There was something unnatural in all the tones and rhythms. When he was alone with his parents they were quiet, but when he heard them during the bridge nights, or at the Bunkerville Tavern, their voices trilled with the forced tunes of good humor, in a conspiracy of pretended gaiety. He felt no kinship. His presence was acknowledged, and his separation; he was the celibate at the orgy, and everyone spoiled him in order to ignore him.

From time to time his father visited the cashier's office, between the bar and the restaurant, and handed David a roll of nickels for the pinball machine. A high score won free games, so that forty nickels often provided fifty games. He stood daydreaming for hours at a time over the garish machine in the dark corner of the dark bar, springing the marble loose, jabbing the flippers at the sides, occasionally achieving TILT. Grownups spoke phrases — "How you doing?" "You beat that thing yet?" — on their way to the bathroom. Goose brought him Cokes, sometimes with a shot glass of extra maraschino cherries provided by Bobbo. Playing pinball gave his hands something to do as David heard, from far away, sounds of the drinkers talking and laughing while his mind made plans for a future of eminence, maybe political office.

In the booth, piles of cigarette butts grew monstrous. Stewie told stories in which he bribed or outwitted union representatives, or hired help for less than it was worth. Finishing a story, he snorted a laugh and drew on his Lucky Strike. Ham occasionally napped with his head on the table, waking to supply anecdotes of his wit in copywriting, often thwarted by unreasonable employers. An old boss from a Providence advertising firm, unjust to

Ham, turned up in story after story, his three names pronounced with rancorous emphasis. "That's the time *Adam Martin Roberts* cheated at pinochle." "The door opened and who's standing there listening? *Adam Martin Roberts!*"

Stewie's face grew redder and his eyelids thicker as the evening extended, but to David he never seemed quite drunk; perhaps he was always drunk. Stewie had come to Rhode Island from Boston, passionate for the Bruins, and hockey provided a lingua franca across generations. When David sat in the booth, tired of pinball, Stewie confided in him: "Montreal is unbeatable in Montreal." "Americans will never be any good at this game." Stewie was a horseplayer exiled south from Massachusetts, where some trespass had made continuing residence a hazard. He hovered between marriages, the only unmarried drinker. Sometimes David heard things he was not supposed to understand, which embarrassed David's father. Stewie commented as a woman walked through the bar, "Take a look at those."

"I think I'll go for crabmeat cocktail tonight," said David's father heartily. "How about you, David?"

It was Stewie who talked most naturally to David, although their subject matter was limited. The war was seldom mentioned, perhaps because the men were only slightly too old for the army. The war hung in the air just out of sight. Sometimes it entered the conversation at an odd angle. "How do you like that Rommel?" said Ham one night. No one knew what he meant. Ham ignored David until he was very drunk, then gave him advice, largely in the form of injunctions: *Always Give a Hundred Percent. Never Let a Friend Down. Stand by your Principles a Hundred Percent.* Ham illustrated this wisdom with anecdotes in which Ham

Heinz, giving a hundred percent while standing up for friends and principles, was betrayed by *Adam Martin Roberts*. David nodded his head at intervals.

By the time Bobbo sat down with them, he was also very drunk. Once he took David to a separate booth because he had words of grave importance to tell him. Drunks always spoke in mottoes. *Respect Your Mother and Father*, Bobbo told David. *Make the Most of Your Education, Be Glad You Were Born an American, Respect Your Mother and Father,* and *Make the Most of Your Education*. David nodded, saying, "I see," and "Yes." On the careful drive home, his father told him that he wished David would listen to *him* with such attention. David explained that he had not really listened, that he knew how to pretend, and that he would have been bored to death if he had really listened. His mother seemed pleased by his explanation.

Weekends they often went out to a family restaurant nearby. Weekdays, when they were not at the tavern, the Bardos had a quiet supper at home. When dishes were done, David's father sat in a tweed overstuffed chair, smoking pipes and Chesterfields and reading a historical novel, maybe a new Kenneth Roberts that the Book-of-the-Month Club mailed, and once a week *Time*. His mother read more broadly, the *Reader's Digest*, Anne Morrow Lindbergh, Thoreau, and Agatha Christie. David walked up and down the room daydreaming, as soon as homework was finished, or sat in another chair reading. No one spoke. Sometimes they listened to Bing Crosby on the radio.

At nine o'clock, David's father looked at his Bulova, yawned, and stood, followed by David and his mother. At this hour his parents spoke, letting out the matters that had troubled their reading. When David's father recounted some anecdote from the office, the story was painful or humiliating. David's mother from time to time told about shopping, something marked down, or how she would soon need to clean the living room drapes. Once in a while she complained of someone who snubbed her because of her South Carolina accent, or because she had married before finishing college and did not belong to the American Association of University Women. His mother cherished hurt feelings, and David's father responded dutifully, shaking his head and making a clucking noise. David's mother patted his father's shoulder when he complained of an office condescension. No one appeared to be greatly stirred, whatever happened.

The point was to get through the day, to eat two crackers with half a glass of milk, then to sleep. Both sleeping and reading, David began to understand, were anodynes for mild pain. Waking from the long doze of childhood, David realized that his parents lived without purpose, their routines accidental. Their whole lives were accidental. Except for their escapes to the tavern, they endured lives of set routine interrupted by hurt and self-abasement — relieved by Scotch at the Bunkerville Tavern.

When David turned sixteen — hair grew on his face; he woke every morning with an erection — the war was over and he told himself that he would not grow up to resemble his parents. He drew away from them, felt coldness toward them or even scorn, while their habits continued as before. With gas no longer rationed, they visited the Bunkerville Tavern three or four times a week, until the accident.

It wasn't really an accident. No one was hurt. Coming home on a Thursday evening from the tavern, David's father drove the car into the garage doorframe. David was standing near, having opened the sliding door, and leapt back without being touched. A left fender crumpled, and the garage needed a new four-by-four —but the accident changed the routine of their lives; thereafter, everything derived from the accident.

That night, they went to bed right away. The next morning David's parents trembled with sleeplessness. Shame still oozed from David's father the following evening, as they sat reading in the living room after supper. He sighed frequently, closed his book and opened it again. A week later he finally spoke, during milk and crackers at nine. "I had too much to drink. I could have killed our boy." Tears formed in his eyes and David's mother patted his shoulder.

The Bardos never returned to the Bunkerville Tavern. David missed the cozy adult coven of drunks, the pinball machine, the Cokes and maraschino cherries. At night he took to staying in his room reading history books—not "historical novels." One night he walked quietly downstairs to hear his mother sobbing. From the bottom of the stairs, he saw her in the kitchen, leaning on his father's shoulder. "He's not the same," she said through her tears.

His father said, "It was the accident."

THE FIRST WOMAN

EDWIN BOLTER was thirty-two when he discovered that the world was a bed. If we lead a life of sexual excitement — as he thought — our lovers have had lovers and their lovers have had lovers also. Going to a revival of *West Side Story,* or to a gathering of the American Society of Statisticians, we see her; and we see *her.* We are episodes in the lives of each other, after all, and although we have not bedded down with X or Y or Z, we have had affairs with women who have had affairs with men who have had affairs with X and Y and Z. The world is a bed.

When an affair began, Edwin liked to tell the story of the summer he was sixteen, and of the first woman. Of course he could not simply blurt it out; no woman enjoyed the notion that she was one of a series. Yet he always wanted to tell the new woman about her predecessors — he reminded himself of obese people who spend dinnertime telling anecdotes of fabulous meals — and he learned how to go about it: When alert skin subsided into mere dampness, when each leaned back to smoke, he would ask her, as if he stumbled on the thought, about the first time she had taken her clothes off for a man. Usually it was far enough back to be made light of. When she had finished her story, he had license to tell his own.

. . .

40

In June of 1945 Ted Bolter turned sixteen, a promising student of mathematics on a scholarship at Cranbrook Academy outside Detroit, a day student living with his parents. Besides mathematics there was the violin, dreams of composing and conducting, of becoming another Baumgartner to conduct his own compositions. He would have concentrated more on his music if he had not worried about the opinions of his classmates. With a diffidence common among adolescents — he told himself, when his old teacher sighed over his apostasy — he cared for the opinions of people dumber than he was; they accepted his presence when he swam a leg in a medley, but addressed him *Hey, fruit* when he walked with his violin past the Arts Academy, the Milles fountain, and the staid oaks, over the bright lawns to his teacher's quarters.

It was this diffidence that kept him from returning to the music camp at Interlochen, where he had spent the previous two summers on a scholarship. This summer he practiced at home, continued his lessons, studied calculus in a desultory fashion, took a girl named Carmella to the movies, and read mystery stories. He was bored. When his mother told him about the chance to visit the Balfour Festival on Cape Cod, he was quick to take it.

Mrs. Hugh Fitzroberts, a large lady in her late forties, had befriended his mother in the thrift shop where his mother worked, and had heard about Edwin's musical abilities. Mrs. Fitzroberts was wealthy, his mother told him, and a patron of the Detroit Symphony, some of whose members spent their summers in the blue air of Balfour. Her husband, on the other hand, was known to care more for balance sheets than for the finer things and would remain in Detroit aiding the war effort while Mrs.

Fitzroberts rented a cabin with two bedrooms near the concert shell for two weeks at the beginning of August, and it would be nice to have the boy for company.

They sat up all night on the coach to New York, the Wolverine, when not even the Fitzroberts name could swing a berth. At first the tall older woman attempted to interest him with intelligent questions, but after they had slept a few hours and awakened disheveled and grubby, their dignities fell away; Mrs. Fitzroberts became "Anne" and Edwin "Ted," and they ate cheese sandwiches as dry as newsprint. At New York they made the connection to Boston, where they transferred to a local, and as they approached the Cape her nervousness started. She became suddenly silly, he thought, skittish as a girl, reminding him of middle-aged men around soldiers—falsely friendly, laughing too much, guilty.

He discovered why. Waiting at the station was a ponderous man, older than she was, who occupied a chair in the Detroit Symphony hidden among woodwinds. They took each other's hands, and Mrs. Fitzroberts glanced back at her companion—her cover, he realized—with a look close to panic: There was something she had neglected to mention.

For the next fortnight, Ted saw little of Mrs. Fitzroberts, who never explained herself and never appeared at the cabin, and although he was shocked he was also pleased. It made him feel sophisticated; he found it a relief to be left alone in a new and handsome place with his music. In the mornings he practiced Beethoven, usually on a quiet beach too rocky for bathing and out of range of sea salt. For a while even the natural world seemed to approve: The salt grass waved in his honor, and the cattails kept time like the batons of a thousand conductors. Afternoons he attended rehearsals of the visiting quartet—they were working through Beethoven, as it happened—and imagined himself a great performer. At night there were concerts in the shell near his cabin.

And there were girls—dozens of young women and few young men. Girls waited on tables, flocked together in boarding houses, played flutes and violas, took notes during rehearsals. Most of them were older than he was—eighteen, twenty, twenty-three. He walked in a grove of young women, lush and warm and possible. He had lunch with one girl, went to a rehearsal with another, ate supper with another, took a fourth to the concert and afterward walked the beach with her and kissed. To each of the girls he pleaded his plea of bed. A few of them confessed to being virgins like him; others warded him off lightly. They appeared to feel awkward about taking a sixteen-year-old seriously. And when each of them refused his proposal, Ted was quick to abandon her, for it meant he could pay suit to another. Every night he went home feeling rejected and relieved.

There was no competition from other males. The only young men at Balfour at the end of the war were crippled or homosexual. (Ted discouraged the attentions of a thirty-year-old piano teacher.) So he dated a girl with a good figure and big teeth who played the cello. He swam on a Sunday with a bank president's daughter, and with a Smith graduate drank illicit beer in a coupe she was driving while her brother was in Europe. For a time he lost interest in music: He was too tired in the mornings to practice. Yet after ten days of frantic dating he had not gone to bed with anyone. When he caught sight of Mrs. Fitzroberts, looking younger every day, the irony saturated him.

Slowly he became aware of the girl in the red MG. Not

many students had brought cars to Balfour, because of gas rationing. On a night in the coupe, he and the Smith girl had counted the miles that they drove. But the tall black-haired young woman whirled in her red MG through the small streets, parking beside the only expensive restaurant in town. Several of the girls mentioned her, annoyed at the ubiquity of the sports car. Then late one morning—Balfour almost ended—he paused when the MG parked at the tennis court near where he walked. The tall girl leapt out and took up singles with an older woman who clerked at the hotel. The girl wore a short tennis dress, the skirt fluted like a Greek column, and her legs were long, smooth, strong, luxurious. She leaned forward to wait for service with an intensity that looked omnivorous.

The next day he came to the tennis court at the same time and brought a racquet and hit balls against a backboard while the girl with the red MG played tennis again. When the women finished playing, the older one walked away toward the hotel, and he approached the tall girl. She smiled at him, and he noticed the wedding ring, and he asked her if she would like to practice with him; when they were tired she drove him back to his room. He asked her if she would play again tomorrow, and she asked him about his music, and she told him that her name was Margaret Suzanne Olson but everyone called her Mitsy. Her husband, Allen, was an army captain in the Pacific, Intelligence, and she was twenty-four. She came from Seattle, and after the war she and Allen would settle nearby in Allison—"like June Allyson with an *i*"—where the Olsons owned the bank, which was like owning the town. Her music was strictly amateur, she said.

The next day they played and had lunch and met for the

Mozart at night and afterward walked on the beach and talked. He asked her how she had gas for her car, and she laughed and showed him a wad of A coupons clutched in an elastic band; her father took care of that. If your husband was overseas, Mitsy said, and there was nothing to do, why not have some fun? Last year had been rotten, really rotten, she said, because her great-aunt was sick with cancer, right in their house, and they had to take care of her until she died. Then she told him about her husband, and their courtship in college, and how her husband was a dilettante at the piano, and they had met at a concert, a soprano visiting Seattle, she couldn't remember which one. And all the time she talked, animated and charming, he thought only of thighs blooming beneath a white linen skirt.

Gulls flew in circles over their heads. He squinted to watch them as they circled, and imagined for the moment that the gulls were spying on them.

Ted asked her if there had been other boyfriends, wanting to keep her close to the subject, and Mitsy laughed again as she told him: Yes, yes, that was what she had lived for at college — because her father had always been too busy to pay attention to her — and really she had been terrible. She had been cheerleader her freshman year because it was a way to meet upperclassmen and football players, and for her first three years she had dated every night, somebody different every night. She was booked for dates three weeks ahead — she told him, and her eyes were brilliant — and on weekends she had two dates a day. Sometimes three.

He felt embarrassed that she might see the effect her words had.

The day before the festival ended, they played tennis again,

the third day in a row. For two nights he had slept irregularly, con-
juring up her strong, firm, welcoming body and then drifting off
into small patches of sleep, only to wake dreaming erotic dreams.
Today again Mitsy wore the fluted white tennis dress, and Ted
was so full of her he could not play at all. He was lovesick, he told
himself, "sick with longing." After a set that he lost, 6–0, she
asked him if he was not feeling well, and he agreed that he was
not, and they drove together in the red MG back to her hotel. In
the lobby everyone scurried about, looking serious and giddy at
the same time. They would have lunch after Mitsy changed her
clothes. As they waited for the elevator, they heard the hotel's PA
system telling them that, on account of the surrender of the
Japanese, the evening Shostakovich and Prokofiev had been canceled, replaced by a ceremony of memorial and triumph.

He felt shocked—as if Captain Olson might walk through
the door and take her away from him. She was jumping beside
him, saying, "Allen! Allen!"; and then she dropped her tennis racquet, hugged him, and kissed him on the mouth. And before she
let him go and fell back laughing, he felt with astonishment her
tongue push through his lips and twist for an instant against his
tongue.

At lunch they decided that the memorial service was not for
them. They listened to the gaiety around them and felt separate
from it. "They don't really mean it," Mitsy said.

He was scornful. "They've seen movies of Armistice Day."

She suggested they have a picnic on the beach, in celebra-
tion. She would collect a basket of food, and tonight while the
other people were at their service, they would sit by the ocean
and drink wine.

She picked him up at five. His heart pounded as he sat beside her, sneaking looks downward where her gray slacks tucked inside her thighs and made a V. She had visited the delicatessen, bought cold chicken, pâté, tomatoes, cole slaw, potato salad, and wine—two bottles of prewar French wine; he tried to memorize the label, but the French dissolved when he looked away from it.

Ted sat near her on the blanket, and in a moment her knee was touching his thigh, and he could feel nothing else. She opened the wine, and out of paper cups they toasted the end of the war. They nibbled at this and that, then confessed that neither of them felt hungry. After a pause in the conversation, after a drink that inaugurated their second bottle, he said, "You know all those dates, all those boys at college . . ."

He waited so long without continuing his question that she said, "Yes?"

"Did you sleep with them?" he asked. When he heard himself, he felt how naïve he sounded.

Mitsy laughed. "Not with all of them, Ted," she said. "Not even with many of them. Some. A few."

He felt jealousy rise in him. "Didn't your husband mind?"

"He was one of them," she said. "He went with other girls, too. Why are you asking me?" she said. She sounded friendly.

"Because I want to go to bed with you, too," he said.

She patted his shoulder and smiled pleasantly. "But I can't," she said, "because I'm married and I love my husband."

"I'm a virgin," he said. He felt himself looking depressed. "I'll get a whore."

"Don't do that," she said. "Don't be silly. There are lots of girls who would sleep with you. I'd love to, except for being married—I mean happily married."

Ted fell silent then, with anguish; and alongside the anguish he felt something like cunning. He dropped his head on his chest. He heard her take another swallow from her cup. Then Mitsy swiveled toward him on the blanket. He felt her arm extend around his shoulders, squeezing. He still looked down, keeping his eyes closed. Then her finger lifted his chin, and he felt her lips on his. This time her tongue went in his mouth right away, and stayed there, and he felt his penis rise rigid against his tight underpants and his khaki trousers. With his hand he touched her breast, or the sweater over her breast, and she moaned and moved so that their thighs pressed against each other.

"I can't," she said. "I can't. Not now."

He said nothing but put his tongue in her mouth.

As they kissed, her hand swept slowly from his knee to his shoulder, pausing near his waist. Then her hand squeezed him through his clothing.

"Oh, God," she said. "I give up. Come on. Come back to the room."

That was all there was, when Edwin told the story later, except for the things that she said, lying with him on top of the sheets in her room. "It's all right," Mitsy said, "because I love Allen so much." And when they first touched, naked, leg to leg, thigh to thigh, breast to breast, her long hair dangling against his shoulder, she said, "Feel it—the *skin*."

The next day Mrs. Fitzroberts appeared again at the cabin, looking slimmer and younger and not formidable at all, and wept, packing her bags. He should be weeping also—he thought to himself—but when he tried looking morose, he felt silly and broke out in a grin. He hinted to Mrs. Fitzroberts about what had happened, and she patted his shoulder. She said that love was the most important thing in the world. As they waited on the porch for the taxi that would take them to the station, among crowds of other visitors standing in front of cabins with suitcases, he wondered how many of them had risen from quick beds. Then a red MG swooped down the road, as he had expected it to, and Mitsy leapt out, shining and untouched, and kissed him long and hard in front of all the people, then drove away, and he did not see her again for thirty-five years.

In 1965, in early autumn, Edwin went to a cocktail party in Manhattan. He had lived there a dozen years, teaching mathematics to graduate engineers, with a specialty that earned him consultancy fees. His host introduced him to a Mrs. Dodge, the host's sister, and Mrs. Dodge answered his routine question by saying that she lived in Allison, Washington.

He asked her if she was acquainted with a Mrs. Allen Olson.

Mrs. Dodge's smile turned artificial. "Yes," she said, "but I'm afraid she's too grand for me." They both laughed, and his host interrupted and introduced Mrs. Dodge to someone else.

So Mrs. Dodge was jealous of her. On the twenty-year-old snapshot of Mitsy Olson, clear in memory, he tried to impose various "too grand" enlargements, a gallery of Helen Hokinson ladies. None of the images endured. From time to time over the years, he had been curious to see her; now he felt the curiosity again. How strange to hear of her a continent away twenty years

later. But the world is a bed, he reminded himself. He had en-
countered again a woman of the past; it reestablished a connection even with Mrs. Fitzroberts.

At this time in his life everything that happened seemed to
make such a connection. Edwin had married in his senior year at
Michigan, too young, and had remained faithful for five years,
doing his Ph.D. and beginning to teach. Then there was an
episode with a graduate student, and another with a colleague's
wife met at a conference. For a year or two he hurtled from affair to affair — inventing late department meetings, conference
weekends, Saturday committees — and gradually realized the
glamour of sexual association. He shuffled in the giant dance,
and mathematics suffered, but he had known for some years that
he would never be more than competent. And music, which his
wife did not enjoy, dwindled to an excuse for absence: He went so
far as to invent a string quartet in Detroit that practiced Wednesday evenings, often until two or three in the morning.

This extravagance was interrupted when he fell in love, divorced his wife, and married again — for six months — a young
woman he loved and could not abide. When he divorced again he
took the job in New York. Cautious of love, finding comfort in va-
riety, he lived in his flat on Ninth Street a life of promiscuous har-
mony — revisiting old girls sometimes, always with two or three
to telephone if he was lonesome — and he searched continually
at parties, in bars, at concerts, at the Museum of Modern Art, for
the faces of women he would add to his long encounter, as they
added him to their own. And many times, as he lay in bed with a
new woman, the light from Fifth Avenue faint through the curtains, he told them stories of his sexual life and sought from them

stories of their own. He told about his initiation at Balfour, and the first woman whose skin he had touched.

Tonight he glanced over the party to assess the crowd, then moved from group to group with his glass, drinking little, listening to conversations. There was a pretty blond woman, early thirties, with the animation of the newly divorced. He passed her over; he wanted no tears. There was a young woman, beautiful if overly made up, surrounded by a shifting group of males and no women at all. Someone identified her vaguely familiar face; she reported local television news and was supposed to graduate to a network. There would be no tears with that one . . . but there would be nothing else either. The men would mill around her all night, making little jousts of jokes and attention, and at some point she would glance at her watch, speak of a morning deadline, and disappear, leaving the men to one another. Edwin found himself seeking out a tall and pleasant young woman, long legs and large glasses, pretty hair, who was eager to laugh with him. After half an hour of talk, he suggested that she find her purse. She did not protest.

As they were leaving, he looked for his host and found him standing with Mrs. Dodge, who was very drunk. "Your banker's bitch," she said to Edwin, twisting the word. "No one is good enough for her. Holier than thou. I wish she'd fall off that deck and break her goddamned neck."

In 1980, at fifty-one, he looked forty, they told him, and when he shaved each morning he tested the flattery out. Although his hair was thin, it was black, and he had grown a burly mustache; with handball and his diet, his waistline remained what it had been at sixteen. His life had not noticeably altered for twenty years, and he took pride in his life, especially as he saw his friends turn fat, alcoholic, diabetic, frightened, and old; one or two had had the bad luck to die. It was true that sometimes he was bored. It was true that the prospect of old age depressed him, and when he allowed it to surface, loneliness felt heavy in his chest. It was true that his love affairs, which he continued to enjoy, had become repetitious. Edwin boasted to his male acquaintances that he had discovered a three-part solution, a relationship partaking of music at its most mathematical. In this solution he kept one love affair beginning, one at a summery peak of attention, and one diminishing into winter. The trick was never to allow two to occupy the same phase, or to allow any moment without resource.

It was boredom, not need for money, that led him impulsively to accept a summer teaching job at the University of Washington. Within a week he had found a young woman who moved in with him for the summer, perhaps a dangerous departure from his three-part invention, but undertaken with forethought. He had begun to suspect that he would marry again—perhaps at sixty, perhaps even closer to retirement. And he had not lived with a woman for twenty-odd years.

Two weeks after his arrival, he found Allison on the map, and on a free Friday morning drove for an hour past hills and rivers and waterfalls through great stands of timber. For the first time in years he felt dazzled by the natural world, almost elated with the grandeur of vista and swoop. Maybe this joy was a good omen for his journey. He reminded himself that returns were always foolish—Mitsy might not be there, might not even be alive—but he *was* curious. The girl in the red MG, the first woman of his life, the social snob of 1965—he speculated on what he would find. He would find a woman fifty-nine years old! Then he remembered his own age, and the boredom of his present life made him shudder as he drove.

He entered the streets of the small town, *Class of 80* spray-painted on the water tower, and found the name listed in the phone book. When he telephoned from the drugstore, a maid's voice told him that Mrs. Olson was out but expected home soon. Edwin represented himself as an old friend who preferred not to leave his name because he wanted to surprise Mrs. Olson. He took directions, parked beside a redwood carport, and walked past a border of irises toward the low modern house. His heart pounded as he rang the bell in the bright morning. Mrs. Olson was changing her clothes, and he waited in a large Japanese living room. Long windows gave onto a deck that looked down a gully to a stream. There was money in the room, well employed and inconspicuous. Three paintings on the wall were signed with a name he could not read.

When she walked in, he briefly entertained the illusion that she had not changed at all. She stood straight and firm, her black hair tied back. Then he saw, as if a film pulled away and he looked behind it, that her face was everywhere finely wrinkled, with dark creases under her eyes and at the sides of her mouth and a trembling looseness under her chin. She was fifty-nine—and remarkable. Her hair was dyed and her figure was trim, her legs a little knobbed with veins faintly blue under her tan. She reminded him, in fact, of Mrs. Fitzroberts.

"Yes?" she was saying. She looked at him firmly, *grand*.

"Edwin Bolter," he mumbled, and gave her his hand. "Ted

Bolter. We knew each other in 1945," he said. "At Balfour. When you had the red MG . . . We played tennis." She looked as if she were trying to remember. He kept on: "V-J Day, Mitsy."

"Oh," she said, and looked pleased, and then flushed quickly with a look that he remembered. "No one calls me that now." She laughed. "Margaret," she pronounced, mocking her own dignity. "I've thought about you. I've wondered so often what . . . My goodness!" She laughed again, and thirty-five years disappeared for a moment. "Really," she said, "I didn't think you would remember me."

"Of course I remember you, and I remember June Allyson."

He told her what he was doing in Seattle, and that he had abandoned the violin because you could not serve two masters, and he told her how remarkably unchanged she was. She told him about her life in Allison, about her two grown children, a granddaughter. There was a child who had died. She told about a return to Balfour, the changes there, not for the better . . . She gave him sherry. She would like him to meet her husband, she said, but he would not be home until late; would he please stay for lunch? She left the room to speak with the cook.

When she returned he asked her, "Who did the paintings?"

She looked pleased again. "Gilbert Honiger," she said. "He's a friend of ours. He lives on a farm west of here." She refilled their sherry glasses. He told her about meeting the woman from Allison at the New York party, without repeating the conversation, and she crinkled her nose when he pronounced Mrs. Dodge's name. Fair's fair, he thought. He liked her style better than Mrs. Dodge's.

Then he began to reminisce about the old summer, and she

seemed happy to join in. He remarked that, over the years, he had come to think that artistic festivals had as much to do with art as checker tournaments did. He was going to tell an anecdote about a Balfour conductor, but she interrupted. "That's what Gilbert says," she said, and made a gesture toward the paintings. "He went to Santa Cruz one summer for something and walked out on the second day." The delighted look was on her face again — and he knew that Gilbert was her lover, and felt a regret he could not justify.

Lunch was an omelet with Gray Riesling and a salad. They talked lightly, and it was pleasant, but he began to feel irritation and loss. He mocked himself for expecting grand opera. They emptied the bottle of wine and she pressed a buzzer on the floor and the maid brought another. He drank several glasses. He spoke of his two marriages. Feeling flirtatious, he let her know that he had not lost interest in young women; he mentioned the girl in Seattle, who was twenty-seven.

He noticed that she had stopped drinking; he kept on. Annoyed that she revealed less than he did, he talked without pausing. He had kept up with contemporary music, and liked it; she had followed it less, she said, and didn't like what she heard. He found himself lecturing as if he were in a classroom, and the more pompous he knew he sounded, the less he could stop, while her smile grew fainter and more distant. He began to feel angry with her, this smooth social creature, Margaret, not Mitsy, who had once clutched him on a beach in Massachusetts. Irritated, he began to be insulting about people who were unable to hear anything later than Stravinsky, and he watched her smile turn cold.

Then again he saw through her dyed hair, back to the luxurious twenty-four-year-old hair of 1945, spread on the pillow of her hotel room the night they stayed together. He wanted urgently to be closer to her, to force her to acknowledge that old closeness, to break through the light graceful surface that she wore to protect herself. Yes, he wanted to make love to her again, and he thought of pulling her up from her relaxed chair and kissing her. Instead, he said, "Gilbert is your lover."

"What?" she said. He watched her cheeks grow red.

"Gilbert is your lover," he said. "The world is a bed. Everybody is everybody's lover. What does it matter? It doesn't matter." When he saw her flush he realized that he was drunk and babbling. "I mean," he stumbled on, "it's none of my business what you do. I mean I understand . . . The world is a bed."

She was looking down at her plate. After a pause she said, "If Betty Dodge told you that, she is a liar."

He shook his head. "She didn't say. I understand about these things."

She laughed. "You understand . . . Why do you say something so stupid? I haven't seen you for thirty-five years and I've been perfectly decent to you. Gilbert is homosexual and has lived with someone named Harold for most of his life. Harold is dying now. I spent the morning with him . . . It was such a beautiful morning. *Maybe* you noticed . . . I sat in the bedroom with Harold, who didn't even know I was there, and watched the sunlight coming through an oak Gilbert transplanted there forty years ago. The sunlight kept getting into Harold's eyes and bothering him until I pulled the shade. What do you *understand*?"

A sense of his own ridiculousness rose to his cheeks and

burned below his eyes. "Oh," he said. "Oh . . . I'm sorry . . . It was foolish . . . I was trying . . ." He could not think how to explain.

"The world is a bed," she quoted. "That's what you like to say, isn't it? Of course it is. The world is a bed, and someone is always dying in it. Have you ever sat with someone dying?"

"I'm sorry," he said. He stood up. "I'm very sorry. I hate to be stupid . . ."

"My daughter's death changed my life. Entirely." She stood up also. "Most people turn more serious when they get older." She looked past him out the windows where the deck hung over the gully. He understood that she was no longer addressing him. "But some people stay children, and when they die they are still children. Harold was like that."

"I'm sorry," he said again. "I'm sorry." Then, as if it would explain things, he blurted, "You were the first woman I ever made love to."

"And you were the last man I went to bed with," she said, "except for my husband. You were a sixteen-year-old boy named Ted, sweet, and I was lonesome. I suppose I used you to make myself feel powerful, the way I did at college . . . and for you of course I was a prize to bring back to school, like a trophy you won swimming. But you were decent enough back then. Now you are an old fool full of self-regard because you still take young women to bed with you. What a life."

He left quickly then.

Two horses stood nose to tail under a live oak, unmoving in late-afternoon sun, in the gully below his car. He drove to Seattle in gathering dusk. Feeling fuzzy with wine, he tried to concentrate on the road and on route signs, but waves of dismay rolled over him like nausea. Back at the apartment he fixed himself a whiskey and quarreled with the young woman who lived with him. Twenty-four hours later she departed, weeping and carrying two suitcases. With relief he knew that his petulance had served some purpose; his mood immediately lightened, shifting to anticipation: On the floor above him lived a red-headed instructor in physical education — with a child, but no husband in evidence — whose muscular calves he admired when they nodded to each other by the mailbox.

CHRISTMAS SNOW

THE REAL SNOWS I remember are the snows of Christmas in New Hampshire. I was ten years old, and one night I woke up to the sound of grownups talking. Slowly I realized that it wasn't that at all; the mounds of my grandfather and grandmother lay still in their bed under many quilts in the cold room. It was rain falling and rubbing against the bushes outside my window. I sat up in bed, pulling the covers around me, and held the green shade out from the frosty pane. Flakes of snow mixed with the rain—large, slow flakes fluttering down like wet leaves. I watched as long as I could, until my cheeks hurt with the cold, while the flakes grew thicker and the snow took over the rain. When I looked up into the dark sky, just before lying back in my warm feather bed, the whole air was made of the fine light shapes. I was happy in my own world of snow, as if I were living inside one of those glass paperweights that snow when you shake them, and I went back to sleep easily. In the morning, I looked out the window as soon as I woke. There were no more weeds turned brown by the frost, no sheds, no road, and no chicken coops. The sky was a dense mass of snowflakes, the ground covered in soft white curves.

It was the morning of Christmas Eve, 1938. The day before,

we had driven north from Connecticut, and I had been disappointed to find that there was no snow on my grandfather's farm. On the trip up, I had not noticed the lack of snow because I was too busy looking for hurricane damage. (September 1938 was the time of the great New England hurricane.) Maples and oaks and elms were down everywhere. Huge roots stood up like dirt cliffs next to the road. On distant hillsides, whole stands of trees lay pointing in the same direction, like combed hair. Men were cutting the timber with double handsaws, their breath blue-white in the cold. Ponds were already filling with logs, stored timber that would corduroy the surface of New Hampshire lakes for years. Here and there I saw a roof gone from a barn, or a tree leaning into a house.

We knew from letters that my grandfather's farmhouse was all right. I was excited to be going there, sitting in the front seat between my mother and father, with the heater blasting at my knees. Every summer we drove the same route and I spent two weeks following my grandfather as he did chores, listening to his talk. The familiar road took shape again: Sunapee, Georges Mills, New London; then there was the shortcut along the bumpy Cilleyville Road. We drove past the West Andover depot, past Henry's store and the big rock, and climbed the little hill by the Blasingtons', and there, down the slope to the right, we saw the lights of the farmhouse. In a porch window I could see my small Christmas tree, with its own string of lights. It stood in the window next to the large one, where I could see it when we drove over the hill.

We stopped in the driveway and the kitchen door loosened a wedge of yellow light. My grandfather stood in his milking clothes, tall and bald and smiling broadly. He lifted me up, grunting at how big I was getting. Over his shoulder, which smelled happily of barn and tie-up, I saw my grandmother in her best dress, waiting her turn and looking pleased.

As we stood outside in the cold, I looked around for signs of the hurricane. In the light from the kitchen window I could just see a stake with a rope tied to it that angled up into the tall maple by the shed. Then I remembered that my grandmother had written my mother about that tree. It had blown over, roots out of the ground, and Washington Woodward, a cousin of ours who lived on Ragged Mountain, was fixing it. The great tree was upright now.

My grandfather saw me looking at it. "Looks like it's going to work, don't it? Of course you can't tell until spring when the leaves come. A lot of the root must have gone." He shook his head. "Wash is a wonder," he said. "He winched that tree back upright in two days with a pulley he set in that oak." He pointed to a tree on the hill in back of the house. "I thought he was going to pull that oak clear out of the ground. Then he took that rock-moving machine of his" (I remembered that Wash had constructed a wooden tripod about fifteen feet high for moving rocks; I never understood how it worked, though I heard him explain it a hundred times) "and moved that boulder down from the pasture and set it there to keep the roots flat. It only took him five days."

It was when we moved back to the group around the car that I realized, with disappointment, that there was no snow on the ground.

· · ·

I turned from the window the next morning and looked over at my grandparents' bed. My grandmother was there, but the place beside her was empty. The clock on the bureau, among snapshots and perfume bottles, said six o'clock. I heard my grandfather carrying wood into the living room. Logs crashed into the big square stove. In a moment I heard another sound I had been listening for —a massive animal roar from the same stove. He had poured a tin can of kerosene on the old embers and the new logs. Then I heard him pause by the door to put on coats and scarves and a cap—his boots were in the shed—and then the door shut between kitchen and shed, and he had gone to milk the cows.

It was warm in my bed. My grandmother stood beside me, her gray hair down to her waist. "Good morning," she said. "You awake? We've had some snow. You go back to sleep while I make the doughnuts." Her words brought me out of bed quickly, and I dressed next to the stove in the dark living room. The sides of the Glenwood glowed red, and I kept my distance. The cold of the room almost visibly receded into the farther corners, there to dwindle into something the size of a pea.

My grandmother was doing her hair in the warm kitchen, braiding it and winding it up on her head. She looked like my grandmother again. "Doughnuts won't be ready for a while. Fat's got to heat. Why don't you have a slice of bread and go see Gramp in the tie-up?"

I put peanut butter on the bread and bundled up with galoshes and a wool cap that I could pull over my ears. I stepped outside into the swirl of flakes, white against the gray of the early morning. It was my first snow of the year, and it set my heart pounding with pleasure. But even if it had snowed in Connecticut earlier, this would have been my first real snow. When it snowed in Connecticut, the snowplows heaped most of it in the gutters, and the cars chewed the rest with chains and blackened it with oil. Here the snow turned the farm into a planet of its own, an undiscovered moon.

I walked past our Studebaker, which was humped already with inches of snow. I reached down for a handful, to see if it would pack, but it was dry as cotton. The flakes, when I looked up into the endless flaking barrel of the sky, were fine and constant. It was going to snow all day. I climbed the hill to the barn without lifting my galoshes clear of the snow and left two long trenches behind me. I raised the iron latch and went into the tie-up, shaking my head and shoulders like a dog, making a little snowstorm inside.

My grandfather smiled. "It's really coming down," he said. "It'll be a white Christmas, you can be sure of that."

"I love it," I said.

"Can you make a snowman today?"

"It's dry snow," I said. "It won't pack."

"When it melts a little, you can roll away the top of it — I mean tomorrow or the next day. I remember making a big one with my brother Fred when I was nine — no, eight. Fred wasn't much bigger than a hoptoad then. I called him Hoptoad when I wanted to make him mad, and my, you never saw such a red face. Well, we spent the whole day Saturday making this great creature. Borrowed a scarf and an old hat — it was a woman's hat, but we didn't mind — and a carrot from the cellar for the nose, and two little potatoes for the eyes. It was a fine thing, no doubt about it, and we showed your Aunt Lottie, who said it was the best one

she ever saw. Then my father come out of the forge—putting
things away for the Sabbath, you know, shutting things away—
and he saw what we'd been up to and came over and stood in
front of it. I can see him now, so tall, with his big brown beard.
We were proud of that snowman, and I guess were waiting for
praise. 'Very good, boys,' he said." Here my grandfather's voice
turned deep and impressive. "'That's a fine snowman. It's too bad
you put him in front of the shed. You can take him down now.'"
My grandfather laughed. "Of course, we felt bad, but we felt silly,
too. The back of that snowman was almost touching the carriage
we drove to church in. We were tired with making it, and I guess
we were tired when we came in for supper! I suppose that was
the last snowman I ever made."

I loved him to tell his stories. His voice filled the white-
washed, cobwebby tie-up. I loved his imitations, and the
glimpses of an old time. In this story I thought my great-grandfather sounded cruel; there must have been some other way to get
to church. But I didn't really care. My grandfather's stories never
upset me, no matter what happened in them. All the characters
were fabulous, and none more so than his strong blacksmith father, who had fought at Cold Harbor.

My grandfather was milking now, not heavily dressed against
the cold but most of the time wedged between the bodies of two
huge Holsteins; they must have given off a good bit of heat. The
alternate streams of milk went *swush-swush* from his fists into the
pail, first making a tinny sound and then softening and becoming
more liquid as the pail filled. When he wasn't speaking, he leaned
his head on the rib cage of a cow, the visor of his cap turned
around to the back like a baseball catcher's. When he spoke, he

tilted his head back and faced me. He sat on an old easy chair with the legs cut off, and I took down my three-legged stool from a peg on the wall. We talked about the hurricane, and he made jokes about "Harry Cane" and "Si Clone." Whenever the pail was full, he would take it to the milk room and strain it into a big can, which the truck would pick up later in the day. We went from cow to cow, from Sally to Spot to Betty to Alice Weaver. And then we were finished. While the last milk strained into the big can, I helped my grandfather clean out the tie-up, hoeing the cowflops through the floor and onto the manure heap under the barn. Then he fitted tops on the milk cans and craned them onto his wheelbarrow. I unlatched the door and we went out into the snow.

The trenches that I had scraped with my galoshes were filled in. The boulder that Washington Woodward had rolled over the roots of the maple wore a thick white cover; it looked like an enormous snowball. The air was a chaff of white motes, the tiny dry flakes. (I remembered last summer in the barn, sneezing with the fine dust while my grandfather pitched hay.) The iron wheel of the wheelbarrow made a narrow cut in the snow and spun a long delicate arc of snow forward. Our four boots made a new trail. Crossing the road to the platform on the other side, we hardly knew where the road began and the ditch ended. We were all alone, with no trace of anything else in the world. We came back to the kitchen for breakfast, slapping our hands and stamping our feet, exhilarated with cold and with the first snow of the winter.

I smelled the doughnuts when we opened the door from the shed to the kitchen. My father was standing in the kitchen, wearing a light sweater over an open-neck shirt, smoking his before-breakfast cigarette. On the stove, the fat was bubbling, and I could see the circles of dough floating and turning brown. When she saw me, my grandmother tossed a few more doughnuts into the fat, and I watched them greedily as they floated among the bubbles. In a moment, my mother came downstairs, and we all ate doughnuts and drank milk and coffee.

"Is it going to snow all day?" my father asked my grandfather.

"It looks so," said my grandfather.

"I hope the girls can get through," said my grandmother. She always worried about things. My mother's schoolteacher sisters were expected that night.

"They will, Katie," said my grandfather.

"They have chains, I suppose," said my father.

"Oh, yes," said my grandfather, "and they're good drivers."

"Who else is coming?" I asked.

"Uncle Luther," said my grandfather, "and Wash. Wash will have to find his way down Ragged."

That morning after breakfast, my Aunt Caroline arrived, and before noon my Aunt Nan. Each of them talked with me for a while, and then each of them was absorbed by the kitchen and preparations for tomorrow's dinner. I kept looking at the presents under both trees—a pile for the grownups under the branches of the big tree, and almost as many under mine. After lunch, Nan drove up to "Sabine," Uncle Luther's small house a quarter of a mile north, and brought Luther back. He was my grandmother's older brother, a clergyman who had retired from his city parish and was preaching at the little South Danbury church that we went to.

My grandfather disappeared—nobody would tell me where he was—and a little later my grandmother was plucking feathers from a hen named Old Rusty that had stopped laying eggs. Then my grandfather dressed up in a brown suit, because it was Christmas Eve, and read a novel by Grace Livingston Hill. My father read magazines or paced up and down with a cigarette. I must have seemed restless, because after a while my father plucked one of the presents from under my tree and told me to open it. It was a Hardy Boys mystery. I sat in the living room with my father and grandfather and read a Christmas book.

By four-thirty it was perfectly dark, and the snow kept coming. When I looked out the sitting room window, past the light the windows cast into the front yard, I saw darkness with shadows of snow upon it. Inside the cup of light, the snow floated like feathers. It piled high on the little round stones on each side of the path from the driveway. Farther on in the darkness I could see the dark toadstool of the birdbath weighted down under an enormous puff of whiteness. I went to the kitchen window to look at our car, but there was only a car-shaped drift of snow, with indentations for the windows.

It was time for milking again. My grandfather bundled up with extra socks and sweaters and scarves, and long boots over his suit trousers, and my grandmother pinned his coat around his neck with a huge safety pin. She always fretted about his health: She had also been fretting for an hour over Washington Woodward. (Wash had been sort of an older brother to her when she was a little girl; his family had been poor and had farmed him out to the Keneston cousins.) My grandfather stepped out the shed door and sank into the snow. He started to take big steps toward the barn when suddenly he stopped and we heard him shout, "Katie, Donnie, look!" Peering out the shed window, we could just see my grandfather in the reflected light from the kitchen. He was pointing past that light, and while we watched, a figure moved into it, pacing slowly with a shuffling gait. Then the figure said, "Wesley!" and started talking, and we knew it was Wash.

It would have been hard to tell what it was if it hadn't talked. Wash looked as if he were wearing six coats, and the outermost was the pelt of a deer. He shot one every winter and dried its pelt on the side of his hut. (The pelts served to keep out the wind, for one thing.) His face was almost covered with horizontal strips of brown cloth, white with snow now, leaving just a slit for the eyes. Similar strips, arranged vertically, fastened his cap to his head and tied under his chin.

When he shuffled up to the shed door, my grandmother opened it. "Snowshoes," she said. "I knew that's how you'd do it, maybe." She laughed, with relief I suppose, and also at Wash's appearance. Wash was talking, of course—he was always talking —but I didn't notice what he said. I was too busy watching him take off his snowshoeing clothes. First, standing in the doorway but still outside, he stripped three gloves from each hand and tossed them ahead of him into the shed. It was cold even for us to stand watching him in the open door, but Wash had to take off his snowshoes before he could come inside. His thick, cold fingers fumbled among leather thongs. Finally, he stood out of them, banged them against the side of the house to shake the snow off, and stepped inside. As we closed the shed door, I saw my grandfather trudge up the blue hill toward the barn.

A single naked light bulb burned at the roof of the shed.

Wash stamped his feet and found his gloves and put them on a table. All the time, his voice went on and on. "About there, McKenzie's old place, my left shoe got loose. I had to stop there by the big rock and fix it. It took me a while, because I didn't have a good place to put my foot. Well, I was standing there pretty quiet, getting my breath, when a red fox came sniffing along . . ."

Now he began taking off layers of his clothing. He unknotted the brown bands around his face, and they turned into long socks. "How do you like these, Katie?" he interrupted himself. "You gave them to me last Christmas, and I hain't worn them yet." He went on with his story. When he peeled off the socks, he revealed his beard. Beards were rare in 1938. I saw a few in New Hampshire, usually on old men. Washington shaved his beard every spring and grew it again in the fall, so I knew two Washington Woodwards. The beard was brown-gray, and served him most of the winter instead of a scarf. Already it was quite full, and it wagged as he talked. His eyes crinkled in the space left between the masses of his beard and his hair. Wash never cut his hair in winter, either—also for the sake of warmth. He thought we should use the hair God gave us before we went to adding other things.

He unwound himself further, taking off the pelt of the deer, which was frozen and stiff, and then a series of coats and jackets. Then there was a pair of overalls, and then I saw that he had wrapped burlap bags around his shins and thighs, underneath the legs of the overalls, and tied them in place with bits of string. It took him a long time to undo the knots, but he refused to cut them away with a knife; that would have been a waste. Then he was down to his boots, his underneath overalls, his much-mended shirt, and a frail brown cardigan over it. He took off his boots, and we walked through the kitchen and into the living room.

Everyone welcomed Wash, and we heard him tell about his four-hour walk down Ragged on snowshoes, about the red fox and the car he saw abandoned. "Come to think of it," my father said, "I haven't heard any traffic going past."

Wash interrupted his monologue. "Nothing can get through just now. It's a bad storm. I suppose Benjamin's plow broke down again. Leastways we're all here for the night."

"Snowbound," said my Uncle Luther.

"Got the wood in?" Washington asked my grandfather.

Aunt Nan recited:

> Shut in from all the world without,
> We sat the clean-winged hearth about,
> Content to let the north-wind roar
> In baffled rage at pane and door,
> While the red logs before us beat
> The frost-line back with tropic heat . . .

She giggled when she finished.

Aunt Caroline said, "I remember when we had to learn that."

"Miss Headley," my mother said. She turned to me. "Do you have that in school? It's John Greenleaf Whittier, 'Snow-bound.'"

"Are we really snowbound?" I said. I liked the idea of it. I felt cozy and protected, walled in by the snow. I wanted it to keep on snowing all winter, so that I wouldn't have to go back to Connecticut and school.

"If we have to get out, we'll get out," my father said quickly.

In a moment, my grandfather came in from milking, his cheeks red from the cold. My grandmother and her daughters went out to the kitchen, and the men added leaves to the dining room table. We sat down to eat, and Uncle Luther said grace. On the table were dishes piled high with boiled potatoes and carrots and string beans, boiled beef, and white bread. Everyone passed plates to and fro and talked all at once. My two aunts vied over me, teasing and praising.

"How was the hurricane up your way?" I heard my father say to Wash. He had to interrupt Wash to say it, which was the only way you could ever ask Wash a question.

As I'm sure my father expected, it got Wash started. "I was coming back from chasing some bees—I found a hive, all right, but I needed a ladder—and I saw the sky looking mighty peculiar down over South Pasture way, and . . ." He told every motion he had made and named every tree that fell on his land and the land of his neighbors. When he spoke about it, the hurricane took on a malevolent personality, like someone cruel without reason.

The rest of the table talked hurricane, too. My grandfather told about a rowboat moved half a mile from its pond. My aunts talked about their towns, my father of how the tidal wave had wrecked his brother's island off the Connecticut coast. I told about walking home from school with a model airplane in my hand and how a gust of wind took it out of my hand and whirled it away and I never found it. (I didn't say that my father bought me another one the next day.) I had the sudden vision of all of us —the whole family, from Connecticut to New Hampshire— caught in the same storm. Suppose a huge wind had picked us up in its fists . . . We might have met over New Jersey.

· · ·

After supper, we moved to the living room. In our family, the grownups had their presents on Christmas Eve and the children had Christmas morning all to themselves. (In 1938 I was the only child there was.) I was excited. The fire in the open stove burned hot, the draft ajar at the bottom and the flue open in the chimney. We heard the wind blowing outside in the darkness and saw white flakes of snow hurtle against the black windowpanes. But we kept warm.

I distributed the presents, reading the names on the tags and trying to keep them flowing evenly. Drifts of wrapping paper rose beside each chair, and on laps there were new Zane Grey books, toilet water, brown socks and work shirts, bars of soap, bracelets, and neckties. Sentences of package-opening ("Now *what* could *this* be?") gave way to sentences of appreciation ("I certainly can use some handkerchiefs, Caroline!"). The bright packages were combed from the branches of the big tree, and the floor was bare underneath. My eyes kept moving toward a pile under and around the small tree.

"Do you remember the oranges, Katie?" said Uncle Luther.

My grandmother nodded. "Didn't they taste good!" she said. "I can't think they taste like that anymore."

My grandfather said, "Christmas and town meeting, that's when we had them. The man came to town meeting and sold them there, too." He was talking to me. "They didn't have oranges much in those days," he said. "They were a great treat for the children at Christmas."

"Oranges and popcorn balls," said my grandmother.

"And clothes," said Uncle Luther. "Mittens and warm clothes."

My grandfather went out into the kitchen, and we heard him open the outside door. When he came back, he said, "It's snowing and blowing like tarnation. I reckon it's a blizzard, all right. It's starting to drift."

"It won't be like 'eighty-eight," Uncle Luther said. "It's too early in the year."

"What month was the blizzard of 'eighty-eight?" said my father.

Uncle Luther, my grandfather, and my grandmother all started to talk at once. Then my grandparents laughed and deferred to Uncle Luther. "March eleven to fourteen," he said. "I guess Nannie would have remembered, all right." My great-aunt Nannie, who had died earlier that year, was a sister of Uncle Luther and my grandmother.

"Why?" said my father.

"She was teaching school, a little school back of Grafton, in the hills. She used to tell this story every time it started to snow, and we teased her for saying it so much. It snowed so hard and drifted so deep Nannie wouldn't let her scholars go home. All of them, and Nannie, too, had to spend the night. They ran out of wood for the stove, and she wouldn't let anyone go outside to get more wood—she was afraid they'd get lost in the snow and the dark—so they broke up three desks, the old-fashioned kind they used to have in those old schoolhouses. She said those boys really loved to break up those desks and see them burn. In the morning, some of the farmers came and got them out."

For a moment everyone was quiet, I suppose thinking of Nannie. Then my father—my young father, who is dead now—spoke up: "My father likes to tell about the blizzard of 'eighty-eight, too. They have a club down in Connecticut that meets once a year and swaps stories about it. He was a boy on the farm out in Hamden, and they drove the sleigh all the way into New Haven the next day. The whole country was nothing but snow. They never knew whether they were on a road or not. They went right across Lake Whitney, and rode over the tops of fences. It took them eight hours to go the four miles."

"We just used to call it the big snow," said my grandmother. "Papa was down in Danbury for town meeting. Everybody was gone away from home overnight, because it was town meeting everyplace. Then in the morning he came back on a wild engine."

I looked at my grandfather.

"An engine that's loose, that's not pulling anything," he explained.

"It stopped to let him off right down there," my grandmother continued. She pointed through the parlor, toward the front door and across the road and past the chickens and sheep, to the railroad track a hundred yards away. "In back of the sheep barn. Just for him. We were excited about him riding the wild engine."

"My father had been to town meeting, too," said my grandfather. "He tried to walk home along the flats and the meadow, but he had to turn back. When it was done, my brothers and I walked to town *over* the stone walls. You couldn't see the stones, but you could tell from how the snow lay." I could see the three young men, my grandfather in the lead, single-filing through the snow, bundled up and their arms outstretched, balancing like tightrope walkers.

Washington spoke, and made it obvious that he had been listening. He had broken his monologue to listen. "I remember that snow," he said.

I settled down for the interminable story. It was late and I was sleepy. I knew that soon the grownups would notice me and pack me off to bed.

"I remember it because it was the worst day of my life," said Wash.

"What?" said my father. He only spoke in surprise. No one expected anything from Wash but harangues of process—how I moved the rock, how I shot the bear, how I snowshoed down Ragged.

"It was my father," said Wash. "He hated me." (Then I remembered, dimly, hearing that Wash's father was a cruel man. The world of cruel fathers was as far from me as the world of stepmothers who fed poisoned apples to stepdaughters.) "He hated me from the day I was born."

"He wasn't a good man, Wash," said my grandmother. She always understated everything, but this time I saw her eyes flick over at me, and I realized that she was afraid for me. Then I looked around the room and saw that all eyes except Washington's were glancing at me.

"That Christmas, 'eighty-seven," Washington said, "the Kenestons' folks" (he meant my grandmother's family) "gave me skates. I'd never had any before. And they were the good, new, steel kind, not the old iron ones where you had to have an iron plate fixed to your shoe. There were screws on these, and you just clamped them to your shoes. I was fifteen years old."

"I remember," said Uncle Luther. "They were my skates, and then I broke my kneecap and I couldn't skate anymore. I can almost remember the name."

"Peck and Snider," said Wash. "They were Peck and Snider skates. I skated whenever I didn't have chores. That March tenth

I skated for maybe I thought the last time that year, and I hung them on a nail over my bed in the loft when I got home. I was skating, by the moon, after chores. My legs were good then. In the morning I slept late, I was tired—and my father took my skates away because I was late for chores. That was the day it started to snow."

"What a terrible thing to do," said my grandfather.

"He took them out to the pond where I skated," said Wash, "and he made me watch. He cut a hole in the ice with his hatchet. It was snowing already. I begged him not to, but he dropped those Peck and Snider skates into the water, right down out of sight into Eagle Pond."

Uncle Luther shook his head. No one said anything. My father looked at the floor.

Washington was staring straight ahead, fifteen years old again and full of hatred. I could see his mouth moving inside the gray-brown beard. "We stayed inside for four days. Couldn't open a door for the snow. I always hated that snow. I had to keep looking at him."

After a minute when no one spoke, Aunt Caroline turned to me and made silly guesses about the presents under my tree. I recognized diversionary tactics. Other voices took up separate conversations around the room. Then my mother leapt upon me, saying it was two hours past my bedtime, and in five minutes I was warming my feather bed, hearing the grownup voices dim and far away like wind, like the wind and snow outside my window.

LAKE PARADISE

ALICE DUBOYCE was David Bardo's steady girlfriend for almost three years, beginning when she was sixteen and he seventeen, in 1947. David had missed the draft, having expected since twelve that he would go to war. He had grown up with war—China, Spain, Poland—and found it hard to imagine what newspapers would write about in peacetime. Now, when he graduated from Grover Country Day, he would undertake four years of Amherst College, instead of letting the navy's V-12 install him on a campus of its choosing. He could think of a profession to follow, after college, without planning for a military interlude or death in battle.

Even the fashions had changed by 1947. When the New Look arrived, Alice continued to wear out-of-fashion short skirts because she came from a family with little money. He liked seeing her pretty tanned legs—and he liked it that her family was poor, so different from his middle-middle-class parents in their suburban house.

They first met when Dave shopped at the Kresge's in Green City, four miles from his suburb of Grover, where Alice clerked on Saturdays. Two weekends in a row, the second no accident, they chatted when customers were sparse. At the second meeting, he asked her to go to a movie. She telephoned her mother, he telephoned his mother, and they went to a movie. He took her home on the trolley, and met her mother, Marie, who was fat and funny—"vulgar" was the word his mother later used—at their three-decker East Green tenement. The place was a cheerful mess, noisy with Alice's younger brothers, loud with a sloppy energy that pleased Dave and left him feeling shy and adventurous; he had never entered such a house. Alice's father, Nate, was asleep in his chair, mouth open, and Marie astonished Dave by asking, as they shook hands, "You get anyplace with Alice in the balcony?" Then she poked him in the ribs, laughing. "Couldn't even cop a feel? I'm not surprised, with this one." She was bragging about her daughter.

Every Friday or Saturday night David borrowed his parents' new Pontiac and drove from Grover, with its blocks of seven-room houses, to the shingled three-deckers packed together in East Green. His parents were anxious, David understood, because their only son was dating a girl from East Green. Of course no one said anything. His parents believed strongly in mildness, quietness, and peace. There were no arguments, only discussions, in the Bardo house. When he brought Alice home to his parents, they were at first reassured. She spoke proper English; she was deferential, always addressing "Mr. and Mrs. Bardo," even calling him "David" when she heard his parents employ two syllables. She must have acquired her gentility from the nuns who taught her in convent school.

They were in love, and Dave continued to enjoy Alice's house with its happy uproar. He learned to relax among the jokes, the shrieks, the teasing, and the high-pitched quarrels. He liked it that everyone was spontaneous; nothing was withheld; no one talked about college entrance exams; no one talked about the future. Marie's sister Joele dropped by twice a week, younger and handsome, to complain that her husband, Freddy, never let her alone. "Every morning, every night!" she yelled over the noise of children and washing machine, rolling her eyes. "I'm worn out!"

Marie yelled back, "You don't know when you're lucky! It's a good week when I get a Sunday afternoon!"

David's parents napped Sunday afternoons while David listened to a game on the radio downstairs. He remembered being given a dime, when he was younger, not to disturb them on a Sunday afternoon.

Joele went on, "He says I wear the rag two weeks out of four. It's the only time I get any rest!"

Every night, if Dave and Alice were not together, they spoke for an hour on the telephone. They discussed names for their children, how many they would have. Alice worried about birth control and the Church. David thought about joining the State Department after college. They could travel all over the world. Alice remembered the nuns telling stories about foreign missions, adventures and acts of bravery, the gratitude of the natives. She used to think about becoming a nun. Maybe, with Dave in the State Department, she could do good works. She could volunteer in hospitals.

On dates sometimes Dave and Alice took in a double feature; more rarely they drove to a roadhouse and danced; sometimes they spent a whole Saturday together at the beach. Because Alice's parents worked overtime when they could, Alice often baby-sat her brothers and Dave came to her house. He played with the children while she cooked. After they put the three boys to bed, they occupied the sofa and agonized about Alice's virginity and possible pregnancy. The nuns had instilled

their terrors into Alice, devils with pitchforks rewarding concu-
piscence. On whom could Dave blame his own timidity? He
cherished her virginity even as he assaulted it on a sofa or in the
Pontiac.

Sometimes they dated in groups or with other couples going
steady. They went out with friends from Alice's high school or
from Kresge's. Dave avoided his acquaintances from Grover
Country Day, whom he found increasingly boring and artificial.
East Green was never false. Often Dave and Alice double-dated
with Bridget Brophy, who had been Alice's best friend from
kindergarten, and her boyfriend, Sally.

Bridget was Biddy — pretty, big-bosomed, legs like pipe-
stems, with long, bushy hair that she brushed one hundred
strokes before breakfast. She attended Mass every morning on
her way to high school, then after school helped out in a conva-
lescent home for forty-five cents an hour. When Dave and Alice
walked three blocks from Alice's house to the tenement where
Biddy lived, they watched the neighborhood deteriorate. They
climbed four flights, over a Paddy's Tavern where Biddy's father
largely resided, to a railroad flat where Biddy's mother was ironing
in a slip and screaming at six younger children crawling among
chair legs. Biddy's mother refused to look at Dave. When he tried
to make conversation, remarking on the weather as his parents
did, she stared back without answering. One night after a double
date, Alice sat in the car while Dave walked Biddy up the four
flights because the building wasn't safe. When Biddy's father
opened the door, ruddy and staggering, he shouted at Dave,
"Who do you think you are?" Biddy shushed her father and
turned red, while Dave burbled his name in confusion. As the

door closed he heard Mr. Brophy yell, "Go back to your own kind."

Alice explained that Mr. and Mrs. Brophy were from Northern Ireland, and that they had been brought up to dislike Protestants. Alice was embarrassed. Biddy didn't dislike anybody, Alice said.

On their double dates Biddy smiled and adored Sally, who was happy to take on the duties of talk and entertainment. At first, Salvatore Mancuso made Dave nervous. Grover was full of people named Stevens and Chambers, and nobody's name sounded like Latin class. By the time they concluded their second double date, Dave felt admiration for Sal. He was breezy, loud, tough, easily affectionate, and handsome — except that his face was mutilated by acne. Cover him with pancake, restore his missing eyeteeth, and he was a crude Fred Astaire, noisy and debonair. He aimed to be a singer not a dancer, although he had one deaf ear, and sang in a voice modeled on Frank Sinatra's. Saturday nights, Sal wore a zoot suit — as out of date as Alice's short skirts — with a keyless keychain that swung from his waist to his ankles.

David wore a necktie, a white shirt, gray slacks, and a tweed jacket. After he turned seventeen, it took him two hours to convince his mother that he could wear khakis in public. All adults in Grover, he noted, wore the same clothes. David's father wore a brown suit to work, a white shirt, a striped necktie, and a fedora; if David's mother took the trolley to shop in Green City, she wore white gloves. They and their neighbors were not rich — the way East Green people said — but moderate in their salaries as in everything else. The difference between the citizens of Grover and

East Green could be measured in salaries: Mr. Bardo made sixty-eight dollars a week toting accounts receivable in the office of the electric company; Nate made twenty-five in the mill.

If Sal astonished Dave, Sal took Dave and everything else the way they came. Sal called him Davey. Sal did not plan, he had no opinions, and it was all the same to him. Dave found Sally's tolerance eccentric and irresistible. When they were briefly alone, while Alice and Biddy visited the ladies' room, they talked about hit tunes, big bands, movies, and baseball; they adjusted contrary devotions to the Yankees and Giants and never spoke of a future beyond next season. At twenty-two, Sal worked eight to five in a cardboard box factory. He had quit high school when he was almost sixteen, 4-F because of his deafness. His debility pleased Sally by resembling Sinatra's broken eardrum.

On rare weekends, the two couples drove an hour to Lake Paradise, where an enormous dance pavilion featured different big bands every Saturday night: Vaughn Monroe, Kay Kyzer, Sammy Kaye, or Carmen Cavallaro, the Poet of the Piano. Presenting their tickets, they held out their fists for an ink tattoo. The MC played a little trumpet riff, walked on the stage, announced that his name was Gabriel, and puffed next week's orchestra. Huge bands hovered among painted paradisal clouds, among painted angels wearing wings and halos on the Heavenly Bandstand. Squads of saxophones, woodwinds, and trumpets rose in angelic military order to play choruses. A male and a female singer sat waiting their turns; one of them rose to sing each song's title phrase. Hundreds of couples clinched and swayed to "Now Is the Hour" and "As Time Goes By." Everything at Lake Paradise — songs, manners, decor — was a deliberate dream. Dave and Alice liked Vaughn Monroe best, "Racing with the

Moon," the amplified baritone riding out onto the plush night air.

David never saw a face from Grover. He saw hundreds of people with gestures and faces that he preferred—Bridgets and Sallies and Alices.

For Lake Paradise, twice a summer, Dave bought Alice a corsage. It never rained at Lake Paradise; it was never hot. Great moons illuminated the lake, with dim cottages on the far side. Couples walked beside the water when the band took a break. On a wooded path around the lake, between dances, Dave and Alice cooled off in the night breeze, kissing, drinking Cokes, and talking about when they would marry. Sometimes the two couples sat at a picnic table and Sal ran through his repertoire, Sinatra *a cappella*: "Ole Buttermilk Sky," "Baby, It's Cold Outside." He sounded handsome in the dark with his blighted skin invisible.

On the ride home, they stopped at a sandy acre filled with dark parked cars. Alice and Dave kissed and squeezed and rubbed on each other, while the back seat throbbed and emitted long sighs. Sal's voice starting in on "Zip-a-Dee-Doo-Dah" was Dave's signal to start the engine. As they left the parking lot, Sal switched to "I've had trouble passing water / Ever since I screwed your daughter."

David's parents suffered quietly and clearly as their son— the A student, first in his class at Grover Country Day, bound for Amherst College, possibly for the State Department—remained in love with a girl from the working class of East Green. David took care to be considerate; if he said he would be home by eleven, or by one-thirty, he was seldom more than a quarter of an hour late. His promptness did not prevent his mother from revealing that when he was late his father's ulcer acted up.

Once when David's parents needed the car, they drove him

to Alice's house — Sal would bring him home — and Nate ambled out. He hadn't shaved, his teeth were out, and he wore a torn undershirt. Nate leaned through the car window across David's mother, and out of his toothless stubble addressed David's father. "Boy! Did I tie one on last night!" He blinked slowly, laughing. David's parents laughed also, patently false laughter that shrank David's spirits.

A month or two later, David and his parents had their argument. One Sunday morning he referred casually to details of his forthcoming marriage; maybe Alice could find a Northampton job so that they could marry while he was still an undergraduate. Suddenly the dark living room, smoldering for two years, burst into dull fire: Did David realize that he would spend his life supporting Alice's family? His mother used the word "vulgar." What would he and Alice *talk* about once they got past the honeymoon excitement? She was a Catholic. Would he be a convert? The priests always tried to convert Protestants. Would they have a child every year? His father quoted Nate about tying one on. His mother delivered a line she had found in *Reader's Digest:* "Washington is full of famous men and the women they married when they were young." Accepting the notion that he would be famous, David felt righteous outrage over his parents' condescension to Alice and her family. He spoke with bitterness about hypocrisy, conventionality, and snobbery. He made his parents ashamed — but nobody won the argument, which dwindled into unspoken hurt lying about in the house's dark places. The subject never came up again.

Dave attached himself more thoroughly to Alice's neighborhood. Graduated from Grover Country Day, nineteen years old, about to leave for college, he worked his last Rhode Island summer on a construction project where his fellow workers largely derived from Calabria. His wages went into a savings account, money for college, and intended not only for himself. Nate had let it be known that college was wasted on girls. In the autumn Alice would take classes at Green College's classrooms over the YWCA. David's summer dollars would help her out.

That summer they spent every Saturday and Sunday together on picnics with long walks, or at the shore. When his parents bought a second car, Dave drove the little Henry J to East Green every night, usually skipping dinner at home to eat macaroni and cheese with the Duboyces. After Nate slouched off to a movie alone, three nights a week when it changed, Dave joked with Marie as Alice cleaned up the kitchen. When Joele called him "Davey, you old son of a bitch," Dave melted with affection.

Twice that last summer Dave and Alice drove to Lake Paradise with Sally and Biddy. Between Vaughn Monroe and the Poet of the Piano, Bridget Brophy missed her period. Dancing to Cavallaro's fingerwork, she wept silently and relentlessly into Sal's shoulder; at a picnic table during a break, Sal forgot the lyrics to songs he always sang. When they parked, the only noises from the back seat were whispers.

When Biddy saw the doctor, he asked her if she had a regular boyfriend. She wept as she told Alice and Dave her answer: "I know who the father is."

In East Green no one mentioned abortion. You jumped from a table and landed on your heels; you dosed on castor oil; you took baths in the hottest possible water. Marie and Joele suggested these measures to Biddy, but nothing availed. Alice and

Dave came for Biddy in the Henry J to drive her to the parish hall
for her interview with the priest. Sal stayed away because Mr.
Brophy swore to kill him. When Dave knocked to pick up Biddy,
Mrs. Brophy flung the door open, her broad face swollen with
tears. She shouted in Dave's ear, "Damn you and everybody to
hell!" In the room's corner Biddy's father sat drinking from a quart
of Pickwick Ale with two empties beside him. "Is that the dago?"
he said. He staggered up and collapsed again.

Biddy tottered into the room in heels, her eyes red, dressed
as if for church and clutching a yellowed white handbag. Her
mother howled, "Whore and bitch! Bitch whore!" She pushed
into Dave's face a framed photograph from the top of the cabinet
radio—prim young Biddy dressed in white. "First communion!"
her mother cried, and sank into a chair as Biddy's father rattled
with imprecations. "I took her to the Easter parade," said Mrs.
Brophy. "I dressed her for the parade." She wept. "She looked like
a girl in a movie."

Father Pellaria answered the parish house door, nodding
without speaking, the black cloth of his suit speckled with ash.
When Biddy introduced Alice and Dave, he shook hands and
nodded again. "You don't have to get married," he told Biddy
when they sat in his office. "Marriage is a sacrament and a life-
long commitment, not to be undertaken lightly. There are many
excellent Catholic orphanages. Many members of the faith, unable to bear children of their own, wish to adopt a Catholic baby."
Biddy and Father Pellaria spoke about a date for the wedding, to
take place in the priest's office. Father Pellaria wrote down "Salvatore Mancuso" and a telephone number.

A week before he left for western Massachusetts, Dave

stood with Alice to witness the wedding in the priest's office, and at Thanksgiving David broke up with Alice. They broke up, they had to break up, it was right to break up—and they broke up with kissing, tears, hugging, and nausea.

The suffering was deliberate. It was David's passionate cold-blooded assumption of class and career. Alice's single visit to Amherst had been agony. She sat smiling and speechless while David's freshman friends made jokes she could not follow. David knew that he loved her and that they could never be married. After the breakup he took the train back to Northampton, to girls from Mount Holyoke and Smith, to roommates who had prepped at St. Paul's and Andover. David throbbed with tears and never wavered in his decision.

Alice became a nurse practitioner, married a medical technician, had three children, and died of breast cancer at fifty-six. What did David become? His record is available in *Who's Who*— a distinguished career in the State Department; offices and titles with years bracketed after them; awards; an honorary degree; memberships; a first marriage; two children; a divorce; a second marriage. This information recounts the passage of the nineteen-year-old who fled from Marie and Joele, from Alice and East Green, from Salvatore Mancuso and Bridget Brophy to Amherst College, Oxford on a Rhodes scholarship, and American consulates in Asia. It neglects to list affairs and betrayals, private triumphs and losses that occupied five decades. Seventy years old and alone, remembering Alice Duboyce, David Bardo masturbates as he lies in bed waiting for delivery of the Sunday *Times*, regretting nothing and everything.

THE FIGURE OF THE WOODS

THE BUNTING FARM is still there, more intact than most of the countryside. In most of this portion of western Massachusetts, the farmland had died long since and disintegrated into stony earth. Or city people bought the old farms and fixed them up and kept them on view like Lenin.

Thirty years before, when Alexander Bunting spent wartime summers there, three other farms had worked the fields between this house and the post office–store a mile away. Now there were none. The Bargers' big house had rotted away; the Luce place shone with aluminum siding, a trailer parked in the barnyard; the Whipples' belonged to people from Cambridge now. Only the Bunting place still looked the same, or as near as it could without cornfields and cattle. Alexander's grandfather Luke died just after the war. His grandmother, a widow for twenty-odd years, had kept the farm tidy and the roofs shingled, but as she grew into her eighties, then celebrated her ninetieth birthday, she had given up her sheep, her chickens, and her vegetable garden. Her knees were too stiff. And now, at ninety-five, she could take care of herself no longer. Speechless, vague, incontinent, old Sarah lay in a bed all day in the home at Hubert's Falls, opening her mouth to the nurses' spoons at feeding time.

One Friday in July, Alexander Bunting, just divorced, picked up his son in Lincoln and drove west to open the musty farmhouse for a weekend. Davis was nine years old, small, and so astigmatic that his heavy glasses seemed to pull his frail head forward. Alexander wanted to *give* him the farm, or at any rate the feeling-farm, and had been frustrated on earlier visits with his wife, Elizabeth—Elizabeth annoyed at the Sears plumbing, at lumpy beds and calendar kittens, at drinking water with specks in it—who seemed to want to protect Davis, as if the farm carried germs that might infect him.

On the trip west, smooth in the old Porsche, Alexander had inquired discreetly into Davis's preferences. Davis's eyesight kept him from taking pleasure in games of catch. He liked to read and had brought with him a stack of Isaac Asimovs, but Davis could read anywhere—Alexander was careful not to speak this aloud —and now they were in the country. Alexander wanted to make his son a present of the past, but a father is not a grandfather, and he felt frustrated: Alexander Bunting who works for John Hancock in Boston is not Luke Bunting, wiry from chopping wood all his life, who loved walking all over his mountain on the pretext of fixing fences, and who talked constantly to his grandson, telling him stories of the old days when the little towns of western Massachusetts, two miles apart and each with its own depot, thrived with an energy that astonished young Alexander.

Davis listened politely, seat-belted alongside his father, while Alexander listed the opportunities of the farm: swimming, and they could get face masks and flippers maybe; hiking, and he could show the cellarhole of the house his great-great-grandfather had brought his bride to; fishing . . . When he started to speak of fishing, Davis interrupted him: Yes, he wanted to go fishing; that's what he wanted to do.

And although Alexander wondered if Davis had not merely picked one item from the list, perhaps the item that seemed least strenuous, still he was pleased. Alexander grew quiet as he drove, and daydreamed back to fishing. He remembered trout fishing the Ben Watts Brook when he was fourteen or fifteen. He remembered earlier catching pickerel from a rowboat in the pond. Earlier still, he remembered a day when he and Luke—Alexander couldn't have been more than ten—had walked a mile and a half, past a corner of the pond, to turn over some hay that had been rained on. Walking back with their pitchforks, over the little wooden bridge where Black Pond became Cold River, suckers poised fat and still in the water under the bridge. Like a boy, Luke couldn't resist. "Watch this, Alex," he said, and he hurled his pitchfork like a harpoon and speared a sucker. Retrieving fork and fish was difficult—but the cats in the barn had a feast that night.

When they reached New Harbor, Alexander parked at the sporting goods store and bought two rod-and-reel sets shrink-wrapped in tough plastic. Then they drove ten miles farther, and turned into the driveway just as dusk filled up the hollows between house and barn. Alexander stared at the farmhouse a moment before unpacking the small trunk and going inside. The place seemed still faintly alive, like his grandmother prostrate in the gray room at Hubert's Falls. He would go and see her this trip, even if she didn't know him. Davis should see his great-grandmother one more time before he saw her in her coffin.

The electricity was off. Davis edged closer to his father as

Alexander flipped the switch repeatedly. Alexander felt panic start in his alien son. Then he realized it was his own panic he felt. Don't let everything go wrong. He remembered that over the sink there was always an oil lamp next to the kitchen matches. In rural Massachusetts electricity was luxurious and inconstant, like the dancing girl in the gold-mining town. He struck a match, lit the lamp, and led Davis into the shadowy living room. Snapshots of uncles and cats, in Woolworth frames, sparkled on tables and threw hovering patches of gloom on the walls. Beyond it were two bedrooms next to each other, with a common door.

The earlier you fish in the morning the better, as he remembered. Alexander woke at seven and tiptoed to look into Davis's room. Davis was reading some science-fiction book. The electricity had come on and yellow light circled Davis, haloing his tender skull. "Let's go fishing," said Alexander.

"Sure," said Davis. "I'm hungry."

Alexander had planned to return for breakfast later, or, more likely, to drive from the pond to the motel snack bar two miles away and eat a big hot breakfast together, father and son; pancakes and bacon and blueberry muffins.

"OK," he said. "Let's see what we've got." In a bag in the car were bread and jam. In the pantry there was an unopened jar of peanut butter. He found the toaster and toasted some bread and they ate peanut butter and jelly sandwiches for breakfast. Davis kept reading, explaining that he was at a good part. Alexander alternated between excitement and discouragement. When he looked uphill to the barn, or down at the narrow boards of the kitchen, or at a frayed oilcloth covering the set-tubs, he felt a surge of excitement. He knew it was a cliché, but this farm seemed more real than Boston and work. Boston and work were intangible, abstract, a conspiracy-to-be-real designed by a gang of adults. This kitchen was uncontrived, accumulated over decades by decisions out of the Sears catalogue. Yet when he looked at Davis, whose thick glasses peered into a paperback book, he was separated again from set-tubs and floor. How could he marry his son to the old world?

While spreading the bread, he had explained to Davis the procedures observed for fishing. First, there was bait. When they had swept up their crumbs—no use encouraging the army of mice—and torn their rods out of the plastic casing, they found a shovel in the barn and proceeded to dig for worms. Alexander remembered digging for worms with his grandfather in a patch of hollyhocks beside the barn next to the beehives. He remembered skirting the beehives cautiously when he dug worms thirty years ago. During the war years, when frequent trains carried tanks and guns past the farm, and cars were rare, they had fished in the pale yellow twilight of July and August after milking and returned with pickerel and horned pout for his grandmother's kitchen and wormy perch for the village of cats.

Alexander sank the shovel into the loose dirt and turned it over. The black clump wriggled with pink tentacles. Davis took half a step back. Beside them as Alexander dug, like a row of shanties in an abandoned town, wooden beehives crumbled in disrepair. Even the bees had deserted, but not the worms. He filled a Mason jar with earthworms and handed it to Davis, who carried it gingerly but without complaint as they walked to Black Pond. They crossed the railroad tracks—one train a day now—

behind the foundation of the sheep barn. In the old fishing, Alexander and his grandfather had used the rowboat, always tied at the edge of the pond, and rowed over the silent, buggy water to secret good places. Without a rowboat, Alexander steered them to the narrow end of the pond, where it turned into the Cold River, to the bridge where he remembered his grandfather harpooning the sucker. Suckers weren't trout or pickerel, in the way of eating, but Davis wouldn't mind. He didn't eat fish anyway.

They found no fish at all except minnows. They stood on the bridge and cast their lines to one side or the other, interrupted only by early-morning delivery trucks crashing up the dirt road to take newspapers and bread to the summer people or the boys' camp on the other side of the pond. After half an hour, a crisp, recorded reveille burst from loudspeakers at the camp. Alexander remembered how superior he had felt, as a boy, to the regimented squads from the camp, hiking past the farm where he had lived to his own tune. Davis was going to camp later in the month; all the boys at his school were going.

"Let's try somewhere else," said Davis. "Is there another place?"

Alexander was pleased with Davis's perseverance. They walked north around the pond, through an uncut hayfield that grew between the railroad tracks and a rim of birch and pine surrounding the pond at water's edge. The field narrowed and turned scrappy. Brush grew in a narrow space between trees and tracks, and they walked single file. Then the space widened and dipped into marshy grass. As they cut down toward the shore, they heard the daily freight rattle behind them, heading for Springfield.

It was here that Alexander had walked with Luke to unfasten the rowboat. After bailing the water that had rained or leaked into the little boat, they slid off into the twilight, in stillness broken only by the sound of their oars slipping in the flat water. Usually they were alone on the pond; sometimes in midsummer a counselor from the camp would be fishing in a far corner in one of the camp's green rowboats; sometimes at the far end near the Cold River they could make out Charlie Ford's boat, with Charlie puffing his pipe into the soft increasing darkness. Charlie was postmaster-storekeeper a mile south on Route 40. Charlie's legs were bad and he brought his crutches into the boat with him; Alexander remembered that as a boy he had decided that crutches were like life preservers on land, which was not exactly so.

And Alexander now, with his young son beside him, walking slowly through scratchy bushes, remembered next his old fear of the pond. The farm women were afraid of water. He remembered his grandmother clucking like a hen about the pond; he remembered Great-Aunt Bertha whose fear was pathological: Women never learned to swim in the old days. He had been warned so often, so heavily—even though he was a good swimmer, taught at the Y in Brookline—that he had learned to fear the lake with a delicate, pleasant, almost erotic fear. There was a drowned man in the water. Years before, a summer worker at the boys' camp, an Irishman from Boston, had drowned one night swimming after work, and his body had never been found. When Alexander ran to the pond's edge as a little boy—first to get to the shore—he looked for the body washed up on the sand. When he fished, he expected to catch his hook on the drowned man and haul a skeleton out of the water.

Alexander and Davis moved close to the water. Their feet

pushed little graves into spongy grass. They found a dry, sandy patch to stand on and untangled their lines. Water lilies lay thick on the water to the right of them, but straight ahead the pond was dark and clear. Alexander cast Davis's line as far as he could and handed the pole to Davis. Almost immediately the cork bobbed with a nibble; Davis jerked on his pole; the cork grew still, small nibbler frightened away. Davis turned and looked at Alexander. "Let's reel it in," said Alexander, "and see if he got the worm." Davis reeled in, but when the cork was nearly to shore the hook snagged. Davis pulled but the line tautened and the pole bent. The hook was caught on something to their right near marshland and lily pads. Alexander told Davis to lay down his pole, and the two of them stepped cautiously toward the hook. Their feet sank; muck seeped in their shoes. Davis made a little whimpering sound and held back. Feeling irritated, Alexander kept on.

The hook was caught on a piece of wood, a long curved piece of timber at the edge of the water, narrowly rising from the sand. He tried the wood with his foot to see if it would bear weight. Then he realized that the wood was the side of a sunken rowboat and at the same time knew it was Luke's; this was the place, the exact place, where his grandfather had kept the boat.

Alexander leaned down and scraped at the sand, excavating a moment of prow. Seeing him dig, Davis inched forward until his feet met the firmer sand near the boat, then knelt and dug also while Alexander told him what they had found. They scraped away enough sand to uncover the iron ring, a bit of rotten rope still tied to it, that had held it to shore. If they had dug further, Alexander was sure, they would have found the lace-rust skeleton of the coffee can that he had bailed with.

Now he loosened the hook and returned with Davis to fishing. They walked back to the farm an hour later. Small perch had eaten their worms, and they had caught nothing to feed the furred ghosts that crept in the barn.

That afternoon Alexander steered them away from fishing. Instead, they rode and walked over dirt roads. Alexander showed Davis grown-up fields where he had hayed with his grandfather, cellarholes of farms that had supported generations of farm families, and houses he had visited thirty years before. On a Sunday afternoon Luke would back the horse into the buggy, harness him —the only work done on a Sunday; dinner was cooked the day before and warmed up—and they would pay a social call on a neighbor a mile or two away, usually someone too old to get out, a frail lady, bundled in August, whom Sarah had known in school, or a blind man Luke had played baseball with. Now the houses were sometimes empty and tottering, blackened with rain and neglect, moving toward collapse; or sometimes a huge family squatted in them and looked suspiciously out at Alexander's slowing car as he pointed to a porch sagging among junked cars and mattresses.

After an hour of loops and crisscrosses on back roads, Alexander turned the car onto the highway. Time for visiting hours at the old folks' home in Hubert's Falls. He reminded Davis that his great-grandmother was very old now; Davis said he remembered. Alexander said that she didn't stand up anymore, that nurses fed her, she didn't wear her teeth anymore, and she almost never spoke. Davis nodded solemnly.

The nursing home was rickety and wooden, the sort of establishment, Alexander thought, that makes headlines: 27 DIE

IN REST HOME HOLOCAUST. Inside, no one seemed to be in charge. Women in bathrobes—and one man—sat in a parlor and gaped in the direction of a television set. In an alcove one group of visitors chatted quietly with a woman in a wheelchair. There were flowers everywhere but the rooms gave off only the odor of hospital—antiseptic and starch and chemical deodorizer, and underneath everything the smell of urine. Then a fat middle-aged woman in white entered the parlor with a pile of newspapers and dropped it on a footstool. None of the old people seemed to notice. Alexander stopped her as she turned to leave. "Please," he said. "We've come to see Sarah Bunting. My grandmother."

"Upstairs, that corner." She pointed. "Last one. She's doing real good. Pretty as a picture."

Alexander took Davis's hand and they mounted the stairs and found the room. Sarah was lying propped up in bed with her eyes wide open. She's dead, he thought with sudden horror, and then he saw an eyelid flicker. Alexander smiled falsely and spoke in a loud voice, introducing himself and Davis. Sarah looked straight ahead and blinked. The room was tiny and bare. Closet, chest of drawers with birthday cards—four months old—arranged on top, bedside table with medicine, window looking out on parking lot and general store. "We drove up yesterday," shouted Alexander. Davis looked at his bellowing father curiously. "Davis and I went fishing this morning . . . Didn't catch anything . . . Heh-heh."

Against the gray pillow his grandmother's face sank slowly back into its bones. A fleshy woman in middle age when he first remembered her, the flesh had begun to leave her when she was eighty-five. At her ninetieth birthday, vain, lively, and attractive, she had looked almost stylish in her black dress and her Newberry's pearls. Now the skeleton showed through, fine old bones under gray wax skin. Bony shoulders stuck out of a blue nightgown, and her small arms lay straight at her sides, veined and raw-looking, ending in the big working hands and large knuckles, still bearing the wedding ring that she had worn for seventy-five years. Her blue eyes, large and miraculous, stared up at him. Maybe she was trying to puzzle him out.

Blue eyes moved and Sarah was staring at Davis. Davis looked back, then fidgeted and turned to look out the window. This must be unpleasant for him, Alexander thought; it's time to go. He began to address Sarah in the special voice, but he noticed her lips jerking in an effort of speech. Looking at Davis, she made a tentative noise, "Alex? . . . Alex?," and Alexander knew that the old brain had found a resemblance. "That's Davis," Alexander said. "I'm Alex. That's *Davis.*" Her lips sagged back into quiet and her stare turned vacant again. "Well," said Alexander, "I reckon it's time we left. Suppertime," he said, and, suddenly with tears, knowing she would not understand but wanting to move closer to this wax body, "It's milking time," he said. "Time to go to the tie-up."

He pulled Davis after him and went downstairs to the car, and they drove to the farm in silence.

Davis was early to bed, taking his book. Alexander sat up and drank Scotch. Saturday night. He began to feel sad, a comforting sadness because it was a sadness that watched itself being sad and pitied itself. The Scotch was ten thousand tiny mirrors. He could not feel close to Davis. Davis was a city child, Elizabeth's child. Which was understandable. But Davis could not seem to accept, even to comprehend—for all his IQ, which his mother mentioned from time to time—this old farm world that Alexander wanted to give him. Davis was polite, of course: Davis looked; Davis said, "I see"; but Davis walked always inside a clear strong shell, like his glasses but thicker, a shell—Alexander thought, as the Scotch warmed him past self-pity into mental energy—made of expensive private schools and poodles named Harold Bloom and piano lessons and recommended reading at the Carnegie library.

Tomorrow they would fish! His brain raced and he felt optimistic. They mustn't go back to the pond, which was as empty as the barn. There was no dark life hidden there anymore—only the skeleton of a boat—and no slim pickerel slipping handsomely through weeds and black water. Again he remembered the Ben Watts Brook, the trout stream north of the pond, a tributary. His grandfather had taken him to it; they had fished it early one morning and returned with two trout that Sarah cooked for breakfast. He felt a rush of enthusiasm. He knew he was drunk, but as always when he was drunk, he knew it didn't matter.

Now he was able to remember the visit to Sarah this afternoon. He laid it out in front of him, as if it were a map he was spreading on a table. The Scotch made it possible for him to think and at the same time to direct this thinking. Well, it was not one of those ghastly homes you read about where senile people were abused and neglected. You could tell that. And after all, she was ninety-five years old. A full life. Then Alexander heard his cliché and laughed out loud at himself.

He looked at the room he sat in. How many years since someone had had a drink here? Or was it the first time ever? His grandmother's temperance pledge, signed when she was twelve and adhered to without temptation for eighty-three years, hung over the bed he would sleep in. In this room old oval photographs hung on the walls — Luke, Sarah, Alexander's dead mother when she was small, Alexander's dead uncle, his dead great-uncles and -aunts, his three living second cousins, and all the cats and dogs. He felt a rush of tenderness throughout his body. When his grandmother died, the farm would be left among five people — himself, his cousins, and Davis. The cousins would want to sell it and divide the money. No! He would buy it; it must not leave the family. He could come weekends from Boston with Davis to go fishing. He could come Christmas, summer vacation; maybe he could take leave from the firm and spend an autumn here someday. No, he thought with sudden strength and conviction, he would leave the firm, leave business forever, and live on the farm himself. He would grow vegetables, keep some chickens, shoot a deer every autumn.

Gradually he drifted into his boyhood dream of surviving as a self-sufficient farmer, Robinson Crusoe of this country hill. He slipped into this old dream and saw himself in a series of pictures: He is writing a book, as he always wanted to; he is feeding the hens; he saddles his horse; he catches a line of pickerel; he salts down fish; he cans tomatoes; his hens lay eggs, which he stores in water glass; he stalks a rabbit in the woods; he sets traps for muskrat and badger; he milks his cow in the twilight.

He slid rapidly and pleasantly through his dream as if he skied gently downhill. Feeling a slight discomfort in his face, he realized that he was smiling from ear to ear. Then he understood that his happiness was only the Scotch and he decided to go to bed. Just as he was turning out the light, he felt convinced that the house was crowded with family dead who disapproved of him: of his divorce, of the silly life he led, of his drunkenness, of his vain dreams. But he summoned irony to help him, and he laughed at himself out loud, and he soon slept.

Sunday morning, and the last day at the farm. Tonight they would drive silently east among all the other returning weekenders, back to Lincoln and Boston. Tomorrow he would go back to work on the new group life contract with Sol Reitman, sitting at the green desk all day. Alexander had wakened with a dry mouth and regrets; he must stop drinking alone. He remembered with disgust his daydreams of living on the farm. What was he supposed to do for alimony? For tuition? But then he remembered his plan for fishing the Ben Watts Brook — and he told Davis, who seemed enthusiastic.

But as they finished their peanut butter and jelly sandwiches, the sky darkened and the undersides of the maple leaves turned up in gusts. Then the wind blew harder and the air turned solid with dark water; wind took leaves from the maple and stuck them to the white clapboards of the house; the lights flickered and went out; the telephone made strange noises; lightning surrounded the house and seemed to walk through it. Davis made a frightened noise and moved closer to Alexander, which allowed Alexander to feel a tenderness for his son that he wanted but seldom felt.

The wind died down and the rain steadied itself, but it was

too wet for fishing and the water too churned up. Alexander lit a candle and dug out the dominoes he and his grandfather had played with, smooth as felt, round at the corners. In an hour the lights came back, and soon after the rain stopped entirely. Sun steamed rain off leaves. Alexander took Davis on a tour of the barn. Then they drove two miles to the motel snack bar and ate cheeseburgers for lunch. The heat turned drier; Alexander wondered if they might be able to fish after all. The sensible thing would be to leave the farm after lunch, reach Boston at a reasonable time, and get a good night's sleep—but then they would have had only their one unsatisfactory experience of fishing, which might sour Davis on it forever.

Alexander understood that, for whatever reason, he was determined to fish the Ben Watts Brook.

After lunch they packed up and loaded the little car. Then they dug worms again. Alexander didn't mention that worms were supposed to be unacceptable to trout; it would have been a long drive for flies; and really, he liked digging for worms if only because it proved that something still lived on the farm.

He thought he remembered how to get to the Ben Watts Brook. Luke had driven the buggy there, quite a distance north of the farm, but Alexander gradually realized that he was past the turnoff. He felt frustration mounting. Seeing a dirt road that led in the right direction, he abruptly turned off the highway. They could give it a try. His head pounded, partly hangover and partly excitement. They drove past a tarpaper shack next to a trailer and a patch of early corn. At a fork, he chose the left for no reason. The road began to peter out; the town seemed to be letting it go; branches scraped the sides of the car and the surface of the road bumped like a riverbed. To the right Alexander saw a flat place where he could turn around and swung in slowly. Davis peered intently over the dashboard.

As he turned in, Alexander noticed two things at once: They were entering the driveway of a once elegant farmhouse, unpainted but still upright; and just ahead the road led to a rickety bridge with water rushing underneath it. This *had* to be the Ben Watts Brook upstream. With satisfaction Alexander turned off the ignition, and the sound of moving water, fast because of the big rain, filled the small car.

"Here?" said Davis.

"Here," said Alexander. "This is the place." From the back seat he took fishing rods and worms and a sap bucket — to keep the trout in — and set them down in the road. He had never seen the house before, and he couldn't take his eyes off it. He walked toward it, Davis following him hesitantly.

It was Greek revival, barely articulated pillars beside the front door still flecked with white paint, a pretty fanlight over the door, newspaper stuck in a missing pane. The land nearby was grown to bushes, but it was plain to see that the farm had been prosperous a hundred years ago. In back a barn had collapsed; maybe an old farmer, making poverty's choice, had stopped shingling the barn but kept a good roof on his house until the day he died.

Alexander stepped onto the front porch, feeling like an explorer, or an archeologist cutting away vines with his machete to find the Mayan temple. Davis lingered a yard behind. Alexander looked through a window at furniture standing in a parlor, dust hairy all over it. Through another window he saw the dining room table, frayed oilcloth on it, with a plate and a coffee cup covered with something white: spider webs? mold? He shuddered and thought of the *Mary Celeste,* that intact and deserted ship that floated without direction on the sea, and of the train men found in the Rockies after the snow melted with its passengers vanished forever. In a few years this house would be another cellarhole north of Tanglewood: a heap of bricks from the chimney, some broken shingles and rotten boards among blackberry bushes. Now it poised between house and no-house, a halo of dandelion seed waiting for the wind or a boy's breath.

With their fishing gear they walked to the edge of the brook, fifty yards from the house. Alexander led, looking for an open spot to cast from. Bushes grew close to the water. They walked between the brook and the collapsed timbers of the barn with its mounds of black hay. They walked past the ruins of the farm shop, forge and millstone recognizable, past a sinking saphouse where farmers had kept fires going under the maple sap in winters of the Civil War. Then everything was bush; the branches were still wet, and their wet shirts clung to their bodies. They found a sandy spot to stand on, the stream dark and moving fast. Alexander fitted a worm on Davis's hook and Davis delicately dropped it near a rock that shelved out from the bank. A quick green-brown speckled shape flicked from the shadow of the ledge, nibbled at the worm, and flicked back. Alexander was puzzled; something was wrong. When he had walked here with his grandfather, he had caught brown trout or he had caught rainbows. These fish weren't the same.

A few more tries, and nothing. Davis pointed upstream and looked quizzically at his father. Alexander nodded and they picked their way upstream. His fervor grew. It was as if no one had fished this stream for years; as if no one had ever fished it before; or as if he were an Indian returned to the land after the settlers died out, after the brief life of the farmhouses, watching the quick water after the rain and the green-brown fish in the water. Green-brown. Alexander's puzzlement returned, and then he remembered something. He stuck his hand in the water, and it numbed with the cold. He remembered Luke telling him about brook trout and showing him an illustration in a natural history book. In the old days brook trout had been native to the streams. Then the farmers came and cut down the trees to plow land, and the temperature of the unshaded water rose by ten or fifteen degrees. The brook trout died off, and the brown trout and the rainbows that liked warmer water took over the stream. Now the farmers had died out and the woods had come back. There were bear again, plundering city people's compost heaps, bear that had not dared to descend from the hilltops for two hundred years. And now the brook trout had come back — these had to be brook trout — under the shade of new pine.

Upstream they picked their way, silent and absorbed, until they came upon a beaver dam. They fingered the workmanship of the new dam and saw the old gray one behind it. Then they pushed through a gate of bushes. Above the dam the brook widened into a round pool. Alexander could see where the brook entered at the other end and pointed it out to Davis. The swimming hole. This must have been the swimming hole for the children from the farms — and Lord knows how many farms there used to be. Alexander and Davis mounted the roots of a great oak, a little platform over the water, and Alexander baited their hooks, and both of them cast into the pool. Neither spoke. Birch trees crowded close to the edge of the pool, and beyond them the dark green of pines over the red floor. The birches leaned in toward the pool and the birch tops gathered together high up, as if smoke had grown leaves.

Davis's cork ducked firmly under the water. He made a faint breathing noise of excitement and reeled in; a vigorous small shape battled him in the water. Alexander put down his rod—though his cork was agitating also—and took a lithe, flopping, square-tailed brook trout off Davis's hook. Davis filled the sap bucket with cold water and Alexander dropped the fish in. He baited Davis's hook again and reeled in his own trout, and when he had dropped it in the bucket, Davis had caught another.

Alexander set his own rod down against the trunk of the oak; one fisherman was enough. Davis let out little giggles of joy and Alexander looked at him with easy affection. The boy's mouth hung open in a grin, and he looked more abandoned, more given-up-to-something, than at any time Alexander could remember. Maybe in two weeks' time they could come back again to this very place. The pool was so beautiful, dim in the woody twilight of gray birch; only a corner of sunlight moved through the frail trunks and twigs. It was as if they were under water and the birches were weeds under water and Alexander and Davis breathed the thick air of the water. I must remember the brook trout, thought Alexander—this cold, old flesh that numbed his fingers was the past returning, the dead replaced by older living things come back from death. For a moment he felt an elation that reminded him of the false elation of drunkenness the night before; maybe, he let himself think, it need not be false.

Davis tentatively baited a hook himself. Then with more confidence he wrestled a trout from hook to bucket and baited again. Alexander smiled—and smiled at his faint resentment, being superseded. He stood on the roots of the oak, floating on his sense of the whole scene: pool, birches, black water. Davis moved on the sandy fringe at the water's edge and approached the top of the pool where the water entered. Alexander was aware that they had to leave soon. Soon they must load themselves up and take the trout home to Elizabeth in Lincoln on the highway full of weekenders returning and drive to Boston and tomorrow the group life contract. But now he stood on the oak's root by a pool in the Ben Watts Brook that was crowded with brook trout and that no one had fished for ages, miles from anyone, years from anyone, and in two weeks . . .

A noise interrupted his thought. Annoyed, he looked toward the end of the pool where Davis stood rigid making a high eerie sound, a small steady keening that, Alexander shook himself to realize, was the sound of terror. Had he caught the hook in his eye? Alexander jumped from the root to the edge of the stream and splashed through the freezing water to Davis's side. Davis was staring.

Alexander picked up the angle of his sight and saw a pile of clothes with a fishing rod sticking out of it. Then he saw the arm, bone mostly, with brown strips of skin sticking to it, a mass of ants digging into the remaining meat of the forearm. The skull was thrown back and wedged between birches, the eyes and the lips gone, a few ants scouring bone and shredded cheek. Through a hole in the overalls he saw more colonies of ants pursuing their labor. One hand that lay loose on the needled dirt was stripped of flesh and lay delicately flopped, finger bones articulate and sensible, still holding together.

Davis turned, dropping his rod, and ran into the woods, loud cries coming from the small body. Alexander ran after him, caught him, and carried the shuddering body through bushes that scraped face and arms, to the car, past the house of the dead fisherman, to the road, to the highway, and east toward metropolitan Boston. Davis lay with face pressed into Alexander's shoulder and sobbed as Alexander patted and caressed him, until after a while he noticed that Davis was asleep.

The rain started again as the car drove itself through the monotony of the dark turnpike. Wipers moved back and forth and Alexander watched miles of returning cars ahead of him, headlights sinking down into a valley and climbing a long hill. Without wanting to, he saw the cars as a line of ants crawling into and out of the body of the dead man in the woods. So he had to think about it.

Why hadn't anybody missed him? Was there a sister or widow alive and incontinent next to Sarah in the home at Hubert's Falls? Was there a granddaughter in Spokane who wondered why postcards had stopped coming? What about the rural delivery mailman, the tax collector, the neighbors stopping for an annual visit on a summer Sunday? Or was there — he realized — no one at all?

So he was the one to bury the dead, closest kin by the accident of Davis's discovery. Maybe one day Alexander himself would die alone and without anyone to miss him. He shook his head abruptly as the mosquito of self-pity buzzed around him looking for a place to land. What should he do? He should telephone or write someone. There must be a constable for the town; he knew there were selectmen. But how could he identify himself and tell them the story without seeming stupid and callous to have run away? Of course it was the only thing he could have done, considering Davis. He let his hand move from the steering wheel to rest on his son's frail neck. Davis's neck and shoulders shuddered like a horse's, and Alexander moved his hand back to the wheel. He knew what he would do; he would write a note addressed "Constable or First Selectman" to the town of New Harbor and tell about the body and draw a map to show where it was. He would not sign the note.

He had solved his problem and heaviness left him. He started rehearsing the conference tomorrow with Sol Reitman on the contract for the new group life. In his mind's small theater he spoke wittily and brightly, and everyone went off to lunch and a pair of bloody marys. Then he looked down at Davis's wet sleeping face and saw that his glasses had fallen off, and he thought how the brook trout would die in the sap bucket in the woods when they had used up the oxygen in the water.

THE IDEAL BAKERY

WHEN I WAS A BOY my father sometimes took me for breakfast to the Ideal Bakery, on State Street just over the New Haven line from Hamden, where we ate the wonderful crullers that Gus and Ingrid Goetz made every morning.

The best memories go back before the war, to the spring of 1939 when I was ten years old, aware of Hitler and newsreel armies marching, aware that war was something to dread. An only child at that time, I overheard my parents' worried talk: My father at thirty-five thought he would be drafted. When I was nine I had collected war cards like other boys, four-color images one penny each in a wax wrapper with a creased sheet of bubblegum pink as a heifer's tongue. These cards showed the Japanese bombing buses in China, bodies blowing apart, entrails scattering in air, but they were not more real than Ace comics. Then one day in 1938 my mother took me to a matinee movie in New Haven, *Last Train from Madrid.* Probably she needed to do some shopping on a no-school day and took me with her offering the treat of a movie; she must have known nothing of the movie. As it turned out, I watched in horror as airplanes strafed refugees pulling carts stuffed with their belongings, their mouths making big O's as they screamed; women clutching babies collapsed with blood leaking from their ears; a father was killed by a firing squad as his daughter watched. When I came home I threw away my war card collection.

Doubtless I was a morbid child, but my life contained many pleasant things. It was during those years that I began to love sports, football mostly. Yale players Larry Kelley and Clint Frank each won the Heisman Trophy. Autumn Saturdays, my mother and I sat on the living room sofa following the game on radio, broadcast from the Yale Bowl only a few miles away, while my father worked in his den on columns of figures.

The spring of 1939 was my last as an only child, for my mother was pregnant with my sister, Evelyn. Because she was restless late in her pregnancy, every Saturday and Sunday we took long rides in the Pontiac. With our car radio my father could pick up WOR, and I came to love the calm cheerful voice of Red Barber reaching us all the way from New York City, telling us about the Brooklyn Dodgers. That was the year my mother began to follow baseball—so that a year later, when she spent her time with Evelyn, and when she had started to act strangely, the Brooklyn Dodgers remained a ribbon binding my mother and me together, not only on weekends in the Pontiac but on summer weekday afternoons as she and I listened in the darkened living room and the baby slept. We heard the names of young players still in the minor leagues—Pee Wee Reese, Pete Reiser . . .

But the best memories do not belong to sports or baby sisters or my mother. Probably the biggest concentration of Ideal Bakery mornings took place while my mother was in the hospital having Evelyn—new mothers stayed in the hospital ten days or two weeks at that time—but the excursions had started earlier, maybe on Saturdays when my mother slept late, and continued afterward, during the war and the long, worried time when she was ill. For six years she was either sick in bed, with somebody coming in to help with the baby, or off in the asylum while help at home expanded to take care of everybody. My father and I went to the Ideal Bakery during these nervous times, but the feeling was not the same. It was anxious wartime, and we were conspirators not in warmth and safety but in an absence or even in danger.

The best memory begins with my father's gentle hand shaking my shoulder in the gray May darkness at five forty-five A.M. After breakfast he would bring me home to get me ready for school before he went to the office. He worked at the lumberyard my great-grandfather Bud had started. Bud died five years before I was born, but I knew all about him: Civil War veteran who sawed up his own trees in his own back yard at his own water mill by his own millstream. My grandfather Clarence built the yard up from a one-man shop until he employed twenty-three people and became "C.W.," the stern cigar-smoking boss (a self-made man, people said), while my father and his brother-in-law worked as co-managers in the office. I knew that my father hated his job —hated C.W.'s sarcasm, hated the maneuvering of my Uncle Bert, Aunt Regina's husband, which always ended putting Bert in the right and my father in the wrong—because I heard him complain to my mother. I heard him weep in frustration. He hated his work so much that he was at his desk before eight o'clock six days a week and brought stacks of arithmetic home every night and on weekends.

But that hand on my shoulder, sweetly shaking me awake, carried nothing but affection with it and tender conspiracy. My

mother, at Grace–New Haven with the baby, was somehow be-
nignly tricked by our adventure, as my father and I performed
commando-like a secret escapade or mission. I dressed quickly
and carefully, tying my own shoes, and remembered to brush my
hair. In the kitchen my father waited in his brown fedora, topcoat
over the business suit always gray or brown, and the shined shoes
always black. ("Meticulous" was a word he loved; he went to his
barber once a week to have his thin hair trimmed.) He waited
smiling the slightly tilted smile — slanted up on the left side of
his mouth with its large skin-mole — that was the grin of our fa-
ther-and-son conspiracy. Pontiac keys dangled from his right
hand.

The windshield steamed those mornings. His gloved hands
wiped clean the glass fogged with our breath as he pulled out the
choke, slipping it back gradually, and we rolled quietly through
the streets of small houses where my schoolmates, never so lucky,
slept until their mothers woke them to Ralston or Post Toasties.
My father grinning beside me enjoyed these breakfasts as much
as I did, and in the early morning he was energetic and optimistic. Often he sang in his high sweet tenor as he drove — "My
Blue Heaven" sometimes, or songs his grandfather brought back
from the Civil War and sang to my baby father, one about "camp-
fires burning" (war in olden times) and another sweetly sad:
"Backward, turn backward, O time in thy flight! Make me a child
again, just for tonight!"

When we reached Whitney Avenue my father accelerated.
Early traffic was light, and we cut over the Lake Whitney bridge
by the long icehouses and headed for State Street. We bumped
over tracks past workers waiting for trolleys and in a mile or two

parked by the Ideal Bakery. We held hands as we walked from the car to the shiny black-and-ivory glass front, then dropped them as we came to the door. Inside, we saw Gus himself standing at the cash register—a red-headed man in his forties, a fierce protective figure, stern but not frightening, righteous and dignified, who welcomed us warmly without smiling and motioned us toward a booth. Always I stared first, to get it over with, at the red birthmark between his right eye and ear, as red as his hair and shaped like the trylon of the trylon-and-perisphere at the New York World's Fair. I could tell that my father admired Gus, in the way that good men find of trusting one another. It was clear that Gus felt the same way about my father, and some of this regard spilled onto me when Gus, in a quiet half-minute, would stop by the booth and say: "Well, look at that boy! Well, I'll be darned!"

The regard that the two men felt for each other, as I assembled it from bits and pieces, had a history that came out of business and bad times. Back in 1932 or 1933, when a nickel cruller or cup of coffee was a luxury for Gus's customers, my father let Gus take some building materials on credit—at his own risk, without telling my grandfather. Gus paid my father back at fifty cents a week until he had a good month in 1936. Then Gus paid the balance all at once, and at Christmas an unordered gross of crullers showed up at the lumberyard for the workers to take home to their families.

When Gus spoke of "that boy"—me twisting, smiling, avoiding his gaze—my father asked about Augustus Junior, called Dutch at school but not at the Ideal Bakery, whom I saw on Saturday visits when he worked with his father. Dutch was a big boy, older than me, who boxed in amateur bouts at the

YMCA. I hero-worshiped Dutch Goetz, just enough older, who worked with Gus as I would grow up to work with my father, making the fourth generation at the lumberyard. (So I thought.) Dutch scowled like his father under his abundant red hair, taller and strong-looking; already at fourteen he carried a dignity like his father's. In four years he would be drafted into the army, if he didn't join the marines first. My father and Gus talked about these alternatives while I listened, knowing that in seven or eight years I would face the same choices; the war would go on forever and I would be part of it.

Gus was proud of Junior and of his daughter, Clara, who was older than Dutch and pretty, a cheerleader already as a high school sophomore, who worked as cashier on weekends and holidays. I could never determine how Gus felt about Ingrid, who was Mrs. Gus, and who waited on tables. I never asked my father about it because I didn't want to ask, "Don't they love each other?" It puzzled me that they were so formal. When Gus wanted Ingrid to bring coffee to a customer, he wouldn't jab his fingers at the cup, the way they did in other places, or call her honeybunch and make people laugh; he would raise his voice politely, moderate his scowl, and say with a rising intonation, "Mrs. Goetz?" I suppose they worked together twelve or fifteen hours a day, year after year; out of character and closeness they evolved this formality.

My young father—it startles me that he was only thirty-five years old—sat with me in a green booth, our hats and jackets and topcoats over the poles that separated the seats. My father's thick white mug of coffee steamed in front of him while I drank a large glass of Brock-Hall milk and each of us ate three crullers.

Oh, the light still-warm delicate crisp gently greasy blond unsugared braids of dough! The first bite was the best, and my father and I looked into each other's eyes as we first bit into the tender sweet crust that "melted in the mouth," as my father put it, and we grinned with a pleasure greater even than our anticipation. When I finished the second cruller my ten-year-old stomach was full but my mouth could not deny itself the third. My father swallowed another cup of coffee, which Ingrid poured while she heard us for the thousandth time praise her crullers. She told us again how she and Gus arrived every morning at four A.M. to get things going, how she stirred the batter just so, how Gus cut the strips and how they braided them together. Then the Greek arrived at six-thirty and heated the oil and turned crullers out for the customers, a fresh batch every few minutes. Yes, Ingrid agreed, they *were* the best crullers she had ever tasted, if she said so herself.

My father and I talked and he smiled without nervousness or anxiety. Those mornings, I suppose no longer than half an hour at a time, we talked about Yale after Larry Kelley and Clint Frank; we talked about the Dodgers, whether Hot Potato Hamlin could keep on winning and maybe stop throwing the gopherball. Then my father would look at his wristwatch and the old nervous or frightened look would come over his face. Breakfast was finished when he looked at his watch. As he drove me back to the house and then to school, we were still good companions talking about the Dodgers (or hockey, or football), but I knew that the lumberyard had taken over.

That's my story, no story at all: A boy and his father eat crullers. Then, of course, other things happen, predictable things. Ancient history is my hobby, and I think of a story Herodotus told, which Plutarch repeated and Cicero: Solon the Athenian lawgiver visited King Croesus, richest man in the world, who displayed for Solon his unimaginable wealth. He expected Solon to be envious but Solon was not: He told Croesus that we may call no man happy until he is dead. Later, when Cyrus defeated Croesus and captured his treasure and chained him to the stake to burn him alive, he heard Croesus murmur: "Solon . . . Solon . . ."

It is impertinent to disagree with Cicero, but I claim that the story makes Solon a simpleton. Everybody knows that the rich and the poor, the content and the discontent, the virtuous and the wicked burn at the same stake. Maybe once in a hundred lives, someone drops dead the day after signing her will or at the end of his active life or without pain or just before noticing the first sign of senility. When this good fortune happens, once in a hundred lives, there is no reason for it. Maybe Solon meant that no one should ever be counted happy—but if that's what he meant, Plutarch and Cicero misunderstood him.

The year I was a sophomore in high school—four years after Evelyn was born, when my mother was still depressed, taking electroshock treatments in the mental hospital—we gathered in the auditorium one morning to watch the school heavyweight boxing finals. (Our wartime physical fitness program had us boxing every day in gym class.) I was excited that day because my friend Dutch Goetz, about to graduate and join the marines, was a finalist. A big blond football player from a rich neighborhood knocked him out in the second round. One blow lifted Dutch off his feet and onto the ropes and he slumped to the floor like a collapsing sack. I had never seen anyone knocked out before, and I was shocked, and I think that my continual recollection of this collapse left me less shocked, six months later in November, when we heard that cottony sound of the school PA come on at an unusual time, and the principal's pompous, somber voice announce with regret that Augustus Goetz, Jr., class of 1943, had been killed in action in the second wave invading Tarawa.

At this time my mother was out of her mind, and I was cared for by a succession of crabby widows while my father looked sadder and sadder and went out alone Saturday nights and came home drunk, as the widows never failed to tell me. Sometimes he drank at home but not often, and sometimes he stopped drinking and took me again to the Ideal Bakery, where the crullers were as good as ever, but now nothing tasted so good as it had tasted before, and Gus's mouth turned further down, and he never said, "Look at the boy!" Sometimes Ingrid was sarcastic now, and their daughter married and moved to Ohio.

After the war ended my mother was well enough to come home, and she gradually strengthened, but as she got stronger my father's head and hands started to shake, kidney failure and uremic poisoning, and he died at forty-five when I was a sophomore at college and Evelyn a fifth-grader. A month after my father died, my mother sent me a clipping about the death, at forty-seven, after a long illness, of Mrs. Augustus Goetz, formerly of the Ideal Bakery. Later I found out that Gus had sold the bakery to the Greek in order to nurse Ingrid at home and had used up the money that they had accumulated over their years of fifteen-hour days. When she died, he went to work making crullers for the Greek, and the Ideal Bakery turned into the Akropolis Café. It's torn down now.

Last week I saw Gus again. My mother, despite her troubles

in middle life, is alive in her right mind at eighty-five. My sister, Evelyn, died last year of breast cancer, and my mother survived even that. But her arthritis keeps her in a wheelchair in a nursing home and she is catheterized all the time. I visit her on Wednesdays and Saturdays; sometimes we watch football or baseball together on a Saturday. I knew from her, maybe a month ago, that Gus Goetz had been admitted, ninety years old and senile. Last week I saw him in the corridor, smaller but still wiry, the same strawberry trylon between his right eye and ear. He was almost naked, the hospital gown pulled up, and he screamed at the orderlies who tried to subdue him, "Shit! Shit!" in a fierce croak. His face and hands were covered with excrement, which he tried to eat.

My mother lives in daily pain, unable to tolerate medication, but her mind remains good. My mind is good also, and although a few physical problems have turned up, I will probably live many years. Was Dutch the lucky one? My father? Not Evelyn nor Ingrid, I'm sure. My mother? All and none, I suppose. Like everybody I live in many places and they are all inside my head. I cannot believe that this is avoidable or that it should be avoided. Several times a week I am ten years old sitting in a booth at the Ideal Bakery, loving my tender father, who smiles across the tabletop. He has not begun to shake; Evelyn is unborn, ungrown, undead; Dutch grows fiercer; the Dodgers look ahead to Reese and Reiser returning from the war; I taste again the twisted light warm dough.

Roast Suckling Pig

DAVID BARDO was driving his wife, Beverly, to the hairdresser in Georgetown when he took a wrong turn. He apologized.

Beverly was dreamy these days, unflustered by tardiness or disorder. At a stoplight, David glanced at her profile. She remained attractive. Her hair, which had started graying in her twenties, had become a convincing brown, and her hips had amplified little since they married seven years ago. "I met a woman at the Converse Club pool last week," she said, "who drove all the way to Newark by mistake."

"Where did she want to go?"

"Pittsburgh," said Beverly.

David turned left and left again. Beverly went on. "You'd like her, though. She'd make you laugh. Alma Trust. She's pretty and she's always doing crazy things. 'Trust Alma,' they say. Once she was thawing a suckling pig in her sink but she needed the sink, so she put it on the roof of a little porch over the side door."

David beeped his horn at a bicycle and Beverly paused.

"Well, the pig rolled off and fell onto her driveway. Their next-door neighbor was a snoopy old lady, sort of crazy, and when she saw the pig she thought somebody had thrown a baby out the window. She called the police and told them there was a dead baby in the driveway. A dead baby! Two policemen came knocking on Alma's door. Well, she was in her housecoat and she still had to roast the pig . . ."

They had arrived at the beauty parlor and David never heard the rest of the story. He and Beverly had returned last fall from Jakarta, where he held a position in the embassy. It had been a difficult year, 1960, when Sukarno dissolved his parliament. It was not a bad time to leave. They were spending three years in Washington, renting an Alexandria apartment, before going abroad again.

William, at four, attended nursery school three times a week. Regina, who was six, enjoyed her new school. David, on the other hand, felt transitory and restless at thirty. He missed the strangeness of another culture, the unpredictable daily problems that kept him busy. As he told himself, he missed his real work. Also, in Virginia they lacked servants. Beverly was an indifferent cook and housekeeper, staying at the Converse Club's pool when the weather was warm, drinking coffee with friends in their kitchens during rainy or cold weather. He felt not only restless but too settled into family and routine; feeling settled made him uneasy. Was this what ordinary life would be like? Surely another foreign assignment would not be ordinary, and maybe Beverly would come alive. Although she remained handsome and agreeable, he missed the lively woman he had married, who was outrageous and made him laugh; he felt put off by Beverly's tepid lovemaking. When David looked forward in time, he did not look to tomorrow but to his next assignment.

He parked near a bookstore where he browsed for an hour. He glanced at books and set them down. *The Sot-Weed Factor.*

Advise and Consent. He noted the attractiveness of the young woman behind the cash register.

Beverly was waiting at the curb, her hairdo as hard as a helmet. When she climbed into the front seat she told David, "They barbecued the pig anyway."

"What?" said David.

"Alma Trust. I thought of something else. Once on a Saturday she answered the doorbell . . . She thought she recognized him as a magazine salesman who had rung the doorbell for weeks, that she'd told to stay away. She said, 'You!' and slammed the door in his face. Well, it turned out to be her husband's boss dropping by."

David laughed. Beverly seemed more animated telling these stories. "Another thing, she likes to read Gideon Bibles from hotels. *Only* Gideon Bibles. People bring them to her from all over the country. She has a whole closet full."

A week later, at a Hay-Adams reception, David found himself looking with pleasure at a blond woman in a black dress who talked with Beverly. The woman laughed, her smile resplendent. In her late twenties, she had a slim figure and small, symmetrical features. She kept patting her hair, as if to confirm her hairdo. Next to her stood a brown-suited man quietly admiring her. Beverly came up to David saying, "That's Alma Trust. The suckling pig? I asked Alma and Roger to supper next Friday. I hope that's all right."

Roger and Alma were half an hour late. "I lost the car keys," said Alma brightly. Beside her was Roger, who remained monochrome to Alma's Kodacolor. At dinner David found himself talking exclusively to Alma. She told him no Alma Trust stories but devoted rapt attention to everything he said. Once or twice, she patted her hair. She was fascinated to hear about work for the State Department and about living in such different cultures. David hoped that he might next be assigned to the Indian subcontinent. There was talk that John Kenneth Galbraith would be Kennedy's ambassador to India. David spoke more about Indonesia than he had done for months; he felt again that his work had mattered. He spoke with knowledge and concern about forthcoming tasks, wherever he was. Across the table, David was aware of less urgent conversation—about Jakarta, about working for IBM, about the Nixon-Kennedy debates, about the Washington Redskins. From time to time Roger and Beverly stopped talking and listened to David as he rose to anecdotal heights in versions of Indonesia, or of his two years at Oxford on a Rhodes after Amherst. Alma contributed fierce heed to everything David said; he felt chosen by her concentration. He heard himself bragging about appearing on a recent *Meet the Press,* "Problems in the Pacific." Modestly, he allowed that he was a last-minute substitute. "Really, I was much too junior. I had to be tactful about Sukarno," he said.

"I'm so sorry I missed it," said Alma with a thrilling smile. "I know it was brilliant. Will it be rebroadcast?"

"Um . . . ," said David, wondering whether he should push things, feeling slight embarrassment over his pleasure in this woman's attentions. "They sent me a tape recording. A little reel thing."

"Oh, could I borrow it, please? We have a reel-to-reel machine. You're going to cocktails at the Willards' on Saturday?"

"Certainly," said David.

"Could you . . . ?"

"If you're sure," said David, feeling a sudden tingling in his testicles, "I'll bring it."

Before the Willard cocktail party, David slipped the small reel of tape into his jacket's side pocket. He followed Alma Trust when she went to the bathroom and waited until she emerged. When she saw him, she produced another smile as she lurched a little. David had seen her drink two old-fashioneds. "I brought that tape for you," said David, feeling awkward. "I think you said . . ."

"Oh, thank you, David," said Alma. "That's a lovely tie. Silk?"

"Shanghai silk," said David, feeling suddenly and ridiculously happy.

"Somebody married to somebody else in the State Department," Alma said, "told me you were a rising star. What an exciting life! I'll put your tape in my handbag." She took his arm and led him to the bedroom stacked with scarves, topcoats, and purses. Her left breast brushed his right arm, lightly enough so that it could have been inadvertent. She tucked the tape into a leather purse and stood with her face close to his. David's heart pounded as he kissed Alma for the first time. Just before they pulled apart, he felt her tongue flick quickly between his lips. She pulled back laughing. "Thank you, David. You're a dear." She walked from the bedroom without taking his arm.

All week at the office David saw Alma's face and felt the touch of her tongue, obscuring his attention to the work on his desk. In fantasy he telephoned her and suggested lunch. Would he look ridiculous? The Converse Club provided them with their social set, and on a Saturday afternoon, while he and Beverly played doubles with Jeff Place and Marilyn, he watched Alma on an adjoining court. David could not keep his eyes from Alma's legs under her pleated tennis dress. In the locker room Roger addressed David: "Alma wants to know if you and Beverly could drop around for a beer."

David's heart quopped. "I'm sorry," he said, "damn it. We have to take one babysitter home, then eat and get another babysitter."

"Are you going to the Bob and Mary Cutter thing?"

"Yes. You?"

"We'll see you there."

David saw Alma before she saw him. She was wearing a green dress with gold trim, gold bracelet, green and gold shoes. He drank two Scotches quickly as the guests danced to Chubby Checker. He watched Alma's bottom twitching to the music, then set down his empty glass and cut in. Her smile heightened. They swayed to and fro. David wished for old ballroom dancing instead of the damned twist so that he could touch her. Beverly and Roger were chatting at the edge of the room.

When the music stopped, Alma said, "I love what you said on the tape."

"Thank you!" said David with absurd vehemence.

"I didn't bring it," she said. "Can I keep it for a while?" When she asked a question, her brow furrowed and gave her a serious look.

David saw his chance. "You could give it back at lunch. Could we have lunch?"

"I'd love to," said Alma. "Samuel gets back from school at two-thirty, so . . ."

"Meet me at twelve-thirty, Monday? The Madison? They do a good lunch."

"I'll be there," said Alma brightly, and as the music started turned her back on David to dance with Roger.

He was working at home on a memorandum for his boss, and on Sunday it was hard to concentrate. He took William and Regina to the zoo, but he was not thinking about zebras. Still, the children's pleasure—an afternoon with their busy father—pleased and distracted him.

Monday, David stood in the lobby of the Madison at twelve-fifteen. When Alma arrived fifteen minutes late, she said, "I'm sorry," with her shattering smile. David admired her blue suit and told her so. "I'm always late," she said, still smiling, and patted her hairdo.

They ordered omelets and glasses of white wine while they spoke innocuously of friends and children. David looked cautiously around the dining room: no one he knew. He grew impatient with himself but couldn't manage to make a further approach. He ate half his omelet and drank a second glass of wine. As they finished and leaned back, Alma said, "I brought that little box with your tape."

"Oh," said David, "thank you."

Alma made no move toward her purse. "I want to keep it for a while, if it's all right." Her brow furrowed again.

"Sure. Why do you want to keep it?"

"Sometimes I want to hear the sound of your voice."

They looked at each other for a long time without smiling. "Can we see each other alone?" said David.

Alma's hand shook as she drank the last of her wine. "Roger

leaves early Friday, for business, a weekend. Samuel will be gone to school by nine o'clock. Do you know where I live?"

David nodded.

"Park around the block," Alma said. "Come in by the side door, where the carport is."

David paid the check. When they parted he pecked her discreetly on the cheek.

On Friday at nine-thirty, when Alma opened the side door, she and David kissed, their tongues writhing together. Alma leaned into the wall of the hallway where winter coats were hanging. A child's hooded jacket fell to the floor. David pressed into her and felt himself swelling. When they pulled apart, Alma said, "I need a glass of sherry." They finished their sherries quickly and made love twice.

The following Tuesday they arranged to meet in the parking lot behind the Practical Motel, on a two-lane Virginia highway twenty-five minutes from Alexandria. David strode up and down as Alma was twenty minutes late this time. They entered room 116 through the back door, Alma dropped her purse on the floor, and as they kissed David lifted her blouse to undo the clasp of her bra and Alma unbuttoned his shirt. They sat on the bed's side pulling off each other's clothes and fucked fiercely.

While they panted and lay side by side, David said, "You're beautiful, Alma."

"Let's always tell the truth," said Alma. "I am pretty. Very pretty. I am not beautiful."

The notion that they should always tell the truth touched David. How many little daily lies did he and Beverly tell each other? How many lies—even "Fine," answering "How are you?"

—did he tell every day? His adultery took on the joy of candor. It was David's first such adventure, if you didn't count a chance Saturday afternoon encounter with an office worker in Jakarta. Then he remembered also the older woman in a Manila hotel, who clearly came to the bar with one intention. "Yes," he said. "Yes. I'm tired of pretending."

Alma smiled warmly. "When we're together I'll say nothing but the truth. For the first time in my life. I've always been a liar." Her smile broadened. They spoke of the dinginess and pretense of ordinary life. Interrupting their honest speech, they kissed again. Alma bent over to harden him with her mouth.

As he was pulling on his socks, about time for Samuel to come home from school, David asked Alma, "That story about the suckling pig . . ."

"It never happened," said Alma. "I *did* set the pig on the roof over the door, and then I thought, what if . . . ?"

David and Alma laughed together, and Alma paused in her dressing to look in the motel's chest of drawers. "Did you see a Bible?" she said.

David asked, "Why do you read them . . . ?"

"I don't really read them. It calms me down," said Alma. "I read where my finger hits the page, once in the Old Testament and once in the New. But I don't pay attention. People think it's funny." She swallowed a pill from a box in her purse. "Shall we come back here? When can you get away? Maybe we shouldn't come to the same place."

"Tuesday?" asked David.

"This time let's get a hotel room in town, say the Carter," said Alma. "You get to the room at noon and I'll call you from the lobby and you can tell me the room number."

David's anticipation was slightly tempered by Alma's expertise.

It was easy for David to take long lunches; it seemed to him that his Washington assignment was largely make-work. He already left the office twice a week to play squash with Jeff Place, an arrangement now dwindled to Saturdays. Jeff, whom David had known at college, worked at an obscure unnamable corporation in Langley. "Pretty woman," said Jeff when he heard about Alma in the locker room of the Converse Club. "Congratulations." His narrow face grinned while his brow creased. "Be careful," he said. "Alma Trust . . ."

David rose to extravagant description of making love with Alma. "She says it's the best she's ever had," said David.

Jeff smiled his ironic smile. "Probably it is," he said, "but did you ever hear of a woman who told her lover, 'You *are* wonderful in bed. Actually, you're the sixth best I've ever had.'?"

David noted that Jeff's cynicism might come in handy. He would confide in no one but Jeff. He needed to tell *someone,* and Jeff had developed the habit of secrecy. Once a week, David recounted to Jeff his latest adventures. After continuing to extol Alma's erotic brilliance, he praised her honesty, and their honesty together. Jeff laughed and responded in his usual tone. "Ah, adultery! The country of truth! The temple of sincerity! The costume of nakedness!"

Alma brought picnic lunches to their trysts in Washington's innumerable hotels. Between fits, they would eat pâté on Carr's Table Water Crackers, drink half a bottle of white wine out of hotel tumblers, or a Beaujolais with Stilton or Brie. Once she brought peanut butter and jelly sandwiches. "I was making one for Samuel, so I thought . . . Roger was right there watching, and he never noticed when I made three, and I used two paper bags!" In her new frankness, Alma's conversations over lunch were confessional. When he asked her, she admitted to an earlier affair in New York when she was first married.

"He was nothing," she said, "but I did a lot of crazy things when I was young. Once I sucked off my sister's boyfriend in a broom closet. I was mad at her. She never knew about it, but I didn't care, just so *I* knew." She talked about the University of Colorado, going to parties with one man and leaving with another. David countered with his two escapades after marriage, episodes at Amherst with Smith students, two strange encounters with Englishwomen at Oxford, a blind date in Rome.

"It wasn't only about men that I was crazy and a liar," said Alma. "If somebody asked me when I flew back to Boulder, and I got there at three, I'd tell them four."

"You never drove to Newark?"

"No. But I did take a wrong turn. In a history class once I knew the answers to a quiz but I copied down the wrong answers from the girl sitting beside me. I was *perverse*." She kissed him. "I still am," she said, "with everyone but you." Alma swept crumbs from the sheet and they went back to bed.

In high spring, almost three months after they started, David and Alma took their picnic to a park twenty miles down the Potomac, knowing that it would be empty on a weekday during school. In addition to crackers and cheese, Alma brought a pitcher, fruit, and a gallon jug of Gallo for sangria. The bottle was a third full, and they felt unusually tipsy when they had emptied it. Still, they were able to return to a mossy place they had found in the underbrush. Walking back to their separate cars, David was touched to see Alma carrying not only the basket of lunch's detritus but even the empty jug. No littering for Alma.

An hour after he had returned home to Beverly and the children, David was helping Regina with arithmetic when there was a knock on the door. He was astonished when William, on his tiptoes, opened the apartment door to confront Alma, who asked, "May I see your mother?" William left to fetch Beverly from the kitchen, and Alma blew David a kiss.

Beverly approached drying her hands. "Alma," she said, "thank you for dropping in."

"I've just got a minute," said Alma. She showed Beverly the empty Gallo bottle. "Last week at the pool you talked about wanting to make a lamp out of a jug."

"How kind of you," said Beverly, and persuaded Alma to stay for a beer. David sat speechless as his two women talked of bridge and skating lessons, summer vacation and children's camps. David was stunned, admiring Alma the trickster; David was terrified and bewitched.

A routine established itself. David arrived at the week's hotel at noon to register and pick up the key. Occasionally the room was not ready, but the hotel would oblige while Alma and he had a drink at the bar. He felt reckless sitting in public with her. At first David used cash. After a few weeks he acquired an American Express card, using his office address. When he registered at each hotel he signed the slip, which paid the bill, and when they were finished he left the key in the room. After school stopped, Alma found babysitters or arranged for her son to visit friends for three hours. She was wholly free when Samuel spent two weeks at a day camp. Cajoling their spouses, they arranged to take their two family vacations at the same time, not to be separated for long. The first day back, they fucked four times.

Roger was never a problem, remaining indistinct and brown-suited at life's edges, admiring his wife and obeying her. If anything, Beverly was even less troublesome — at the Converse Club pool with the children, visiting her women friends, undemanding in bed. David noted that he paid less attention to Regina and William. He tried to make it up by watching *Leave It to Beaver* with them, laughing when they laughed. Once the Bardos and the Trusts went to *Jules et Jim* together. David and Alma managed to touch once. Their love affair seemed stable and perpetual — except that his next foreign assignment lay ahead, seldom mentioned by either of them. They spoke of a marriage after twin divorces but dismissed the notion because of the children. David daydreamed trysts in Ceylon, trips back to the United States for consultation.

They never quarreled, or almost never. At one of their assignations, Alma refused David's suggested next meeting because it would require her to break a tennis date with friends. It was a week of conferences for David, and Tuesday was the only possible day for a rendezvous. He was hurt, and mumbled that he supposed tennis was more important than he was. Alma retaliated by mentioning the lovemaking athleticism of a college boyfriend, and David's stomach went hollow. He lapsed into sullen silence, and Alma left after only one time.

A month later, after school had started again, Alma called David one morning at the office, which she was not to do, and told him she was sorry but she couldn't meet him at the Clinton that noon as planned. An old college roommate, whom she had not seen for years, had a two-hour layover at National, and Alma *had* to see her. Controlling his fury, David suggested that they tryst two days hence. Alma agreed. David changed the room reservation and kept his rage intact for forty-eight hours until Alma, smiling sweetly, entered the hotel room. They went to bed immediately — angry sex for David — and when they lay back to recover he let her know that breaking dates for friends laying over at National was not to be tolerated.

Alma laughed and teased, but David felt underneath her surface a counter-rage which she kept under control. "You're so possessive," she said. "Try to let up a little. Max was like that."

"Max?" said David.

"I lied to you once," said Alma. "It's the only lie I ever told you. I know we agreed to tell the truth. I'm sorry. I knew it would upset you."

"Who's Max?"

"I told you I'd had only one affair, in New York, but really I had one in Washington three years ago with Max Freitas, F-r-e-i-t-a-s. He's a law professor at Georgetown. Maybe you met him at some party? It didn't last long. We met at hotels like this."

David felt as though his 707 had dropped ten thousand feet in ten seconds. He remembered no Max Freitas. "You *lied* to me," he said. Dimly he understood that her lying gave her power over him. He felt possessed, at the same time giddy with rage and with passion. Alma looked at him steadily and seriously with a faint version of her smile.

"I liked him at first but he was *so* possessive. I couldn't *move* without telling him what I was doing. Finally I couldn't stand it anymore."

"How many times did you see him?" David's heart thumped in his chest. Alma began to look angry as he asked more questions. She opened a Gideon and hurled it down without reading from it. She dressed quickly and hurried to the door with her head held high. David sprawled naked on the bed, weeping and outraged, calling after her as she left, "Did you go to the same hotels?"

"You're disgusting," said Alma. "I *refuse* to listen." She slammed the door.

David was heavy-hearted and quarreled with Beverly when she left him with Regina and William on Sunday; her friend Eloise had a problem and needed to talk. After she left, William wanted to watch cartoons, and Regina the Redskins. The children squabbled until David shut off the TV and sent them to their rooms howling. He read the *Times* as well as the *Post*. He tried to study statistics about the Asian economy. When Beverly returned, they ate dinner in silence, and after the children were in bed accused each other of having changed utterly since Jakarta.

The next day, as David sat at his desk missing Alma, angry at Alma, she telephoned again. She was heartsick, she said, and must see him now. She would meet him at noon at the Practical Motel, their first secret place. She had something important to tell him. Very important.

Despite his anger, David's heart pounded again. Uncomfortably, he told his assistant that something pressing necessitated his departure, and telephoned the motel from the street. He was early, Alma was late, but they fell into each other's arms in the parking lot before he opened the door. She sat on the bed and he tried to kiss her, horny and furious. She pushed him away. "Not yet. I have to tell you something."

David feared what he would hear. Alma looked him beautifully in the eyes and spoke with calm candor. "David, I'm sorry. I'm so sorry. I lied to you. It's the only time, David, and I'll never do it again."

David felt bewildered.

"I was angry. I lied to you. I never had an affair with Max Freitas. Never once. I knew him, he flirted with me, but we never went to bed. I promise, promise." She patted her hair, and David realized that she had mostly stopped patting her hair.

Alma was convincing, but Alma had been convincing the Friday before. "I'll never lie to you again. I'm sorry, David! And I can prove it." She reached into her handbag and took out a crinkled newspaper clipping. She did not smile, and her brow was deeply furrowed. "I told you it happened three years ago?" David looked at the photograph of a frowning man, a headline that announced that Dr. Max Freitas would take up his duties as visiting professor in Frankfurt, leaving Georgetown for a period of eighteen months—and the date over the clipping was four years back. "I saved the clipping to give it to him, back before he went away—we saw each other when I took those classes at Georgetown—but I never saw him again, to give it to him. I don't think I've seen him since I stopped taking classes and he went to Frankfurt. I found this clipping a week ago, which is why I thought about him when I was mad at you. See, he was gone *just* when I told you we were having an affair."

David read the date again, and then the clipping again. "You sounded so sincere," he said. "I totally believed you. You scare me. Why should I believe you now?"

"I've always been able to do it. I scare myself. David, *David*, I'll never do it again!" She unbuttoned his shirt.

When David told Jeff this story, Jeff was speechless for once. He shook his head and looked at David. He started to speak and stopped.

As the Washington winter approached, David spoke idly one afternoon as he and Alma dressed in their hotel room. "Dark, dark. I wish we could fly off to get some sun somewhere."

"Let's," said Alma.

"How?" said David.

"Beverly hasn't noticed anything. Roger never notices anything. Can't you take a week away? Sick leave . . . or something?"

David nodded. "But you . . . ?"

Alma picked up a Bible, leafing through, then smiled as broadly as when she had brought Beverly the gallon jug. "My best friend in college, my old roommate Simone, the one I went to see at National? Her family has a hunting lodge in the mountains near Palm Springs. Without a telephone."

"You mean, we can go there? Is it warm?"

"Warm enough to be an excuse. We can fly to Key West, which is closer, and call home once a day, saying—or I can say— that I drove to a pay phone." David had never seen Alma look so pleased. "Of course, we could go to California, but it would be more fun to be someplace else."

He made reservations for early in December at an oceanfront motel in Key West. Suppose they saw someone they knew? He felt mild anxiety over his work, over Beverly and the children — as he thrilled with adventure. What would Alma come up with next? Panic returned for a moment.

He arranged for the time off with his superior and explained to Beverly that he needed to attend a conference rather confidential in its nature. She seemed to take little interest. These days, when David telephoned her at home, she seldom answered. Could Beverly also be having an affair? The notion passed, after a flash of jealousy, without leaving residue.

Alma and David flew together into sunshine, a warm pool, and sandy beaches. They played tennis, lay on the sand, visited shops largely empty, ate well, went to see *Days of Wine and Roses*, and made love three times a day. Southern California would explain Alma's tan, and David had intimated to Beverly that his conference was taking him south. Their idyll was interrupted by brief separations when each of them talked long-distance to children and spouses. These calls left David melancholy at first. "When are you coming home, Daddy?" said William. Regina sounded distant and Beverly more distant still. Then the calls pleased him — as they did Alma — by their fraudulence.

Their long holiday together was perfect happiness, unshaken by the absence of a Gideon Bible. The day before they flew home, Alma had a new idea: Each would make the required telephone call, but from their own illicit room while the other listened. Alma went first, dialing her husband at evening when she knew he would be cooking. Samuel answered, and Alma smiled sweetly as she lay naked beside David, asking about the spelling test. She listened, saying, "Yes," "My goodness," "She did?" —

until she had to interrupt: "Please put Daddy on the phone." David overheard a daddy clearly harassed, making hamburgers because Sammy was tired of pizza, and he hoped she was having a good time in that damned hunting lodge. As she talked to Roger, Alma's left hand reached over to stroke David's penis swiftly and more swiftly. "Well, I'll be home late tomorrow," Alma told him. "Tell Samuel I love him."

When she hung up she remarked that David would have to wait before he called Beverly.

When Alma and David returned from Key West, David felt more obsessed than ever. Adventures in deceit were tender as well as aphrodisiac. One day Alma declared that these hotel rooms made her sick. "Let's buy a house."

David gasped. "Well," said Alma, "we could rent a room somewhere. Where no one knows us. I could make it pretty. We could meet more often, almost every day."

What Alma wanted, David procured. Once again he wondered whether he was in love or under a spell. He remembered the time, not long ago, when he thrived under the spell of his State Department work. He found a flat, double bed and kitchenette, in a student neighborhood near American University. The landlord lived a block away; students would pay no attention to random appearances of a middle-aged couple obviously too old for sex. David showed Alma the flat, to ask if she approved. "I'll make new curtains," said Alma, frowning. "These are hideous. I'll put the little Cassatt print there. Roger will never miss it. Let's call it Love Nest, the way the tabloids do."

David rented under the name of Leo Pious; Alma was a lapsed Catholic. With a check from a new bank account in Leo's name, David paid the first and last month's rent. Whenever he did anything cleverly duplicitous, Alma praised him with enthusiasm. Now they met almost daily at eleven-thirty or twelve, went to bed, ate the cheese or pâté that Alma kept in the refrigerator, went to bed again, and parted. She no longer patted her hair. "Your hair is so soft," said David.

Alma smiled. "I never spray it now," she said, "except sometimes for a party." She paused. "It feels better when you touch it."

When she was menstruating, usually Alma sucked David off; at other times, they let things get a little messy. Sometimes Alma had to meet women friends, or her friends might suspect. David's long lunch breaks were noted, but he finished the work assigned him.

After Saturday squash at the Converse Club, David talked with Jeff about Alma. These days, David spoke less about the lovemaking and more about the escapades, the tricks Alma played. Once, David concluded, "Affairs require trickery."

Jeff smiled. "Maybe trickery requires affairs," he said.

The remark puzzled David. Then he remembered the Gallo jug, Key West, and Love Nest. "Maybe you're right. Maybe I'm possessed by the secrecy, the danger. It makes the sex better."

"You're possessed by *something*." Jeff sighed, wiping his creased forehead with a towel. "It reminds me of my business," he said.

"What?" said David.

"False identities and documents, codes, drop spots. You and Alma are like an underground cell, plotting against the government. Don't think plotters don't enjoy their peril. Danger salts the meat of everyday life: surreptitiousness, close calls, getting away with it. It's no secret that I spent two years in West Berlin, in contact with anti-regime people from the East. Maybe that's why I'm faithful to Marilyn. My East Germans were always conspiring, always in danger. None of them had love affairs."

Friday and Saturday afternoons, or on Sunday after tennis, Alma and David attended the same cocktail parties. Each of them arrived and left with a spouse, and in between they drank and danced with their social set. Barbra Streisand on the hi-fi. These men and women played bridge and tennis together, and their children visited each other after school. Alma and David agreed that no one suspected them. Sometimes they managed to fondle in a dark bedroom; once they went down on each other in an attic.

Often two or three couples would begin a Saturday night at one party and drive to another, and maybe yet another. Once Alma suggested that the Bardos and the Trusts switch places for the drive from one house to another. Beverly and Roger drove off together. David opened the car door for Alma, who had forgotten her scarf and returned to the hallway to find it. When they drove off Alma said, "I didn't forget my scarf."

"Why did you . . . ?"

"I wanted them to get a head start. We drive by Love Nest on the way to Bernie's."

"What will we tell them?"

"I'll say I was navigator and we got lost. Everybody will believe me." At Love Nest they were quick.

After two years had passed they began to quarrel. It was six months before the Bardos would fly to Bombay, and Bombay annoyed Alma. They spoke again of double divorces and again dismissed the notion. Alma didn't want to go to India. David spoke of schemes by which he and Alma could spend a week in Paris or Tokyo, and assured her that his work would require a return to Washington at least twice a year. Alma told him that if he took the assignment in Bombay, it meant that he didn't love her. David answered that if he didn't take the assignment, it would be the end of his career.

"Career!" said Alma. "Roger likes to talk about *careers*."

Increasingly, Alma canceled visits to Love Nest. Increasingly, she picked up a Gideon Bible she had secreted under the bed. After two absences in a row, David met her at Leo Pious's door in a fury. Alma raised her voice—about possessiveness, about Bombay—and walked out saying, "That's *that!*" David remained in the room, trembling and heartsick. Twenty minutes later Alma opened the door weeping and threw herself into David's arms. The next day she brought with her the ingredients and mixer for making mayonnaise. David went so far as to inquire of a superior if it might not be possible for him to remain in Washington. As he entered his superior's office, he found himself remembering the time Alma and Roger came to dinner, the intensity with which he had talked about his work in Indonesia.

It was not possible. A week later David and Alma broke up again. After two days Alma called him at the forbidden office, teary and contrite. They came back together again, then broke up again. David understood—in panic and with something like relief—that the affair was going to end. He *had* to go to Bombay. He said as much to Jeff, who shrugged and patted David's back. "Take it easy," said Jeff.

To finish it once and for all, Alma confessed to Roger. Roger was nature's cuckold, as David understood, fated to marry a beautiful woman who would have his child and a sequence of lovers. Roger would know, but he would not know he knew. Alma told David over the telephone that when she confessed, Roger was profoundly shocked, and made her promise to stop seeing David or he would divorce her and sue for custody of Samuel. The breakup was final. After two weeks without telephone calls, David emptied out Love Nest. He kept the small Cassatt in a filing cabinet. He enjoyed keeping the Cassatt.

A month later, David had immersed himself in studying Hindi at the Foreign Service Institute. On a Saturday night he watched Alma from a distance at an Alexandria cocktail party as she listened intently to a broker of David's acquaintance who was clearly lovesick. She patted her tight hairdo. Soon enough, he heard Alma Trust stories again—how she locked herself out of the house wearing nothing but a bikini bottom. He listened attentively, as if the stories were history, and felt wistful and enraged. He tried imagining life in Bombay with Beverly and the children.

Not long before their scheduled departure, Beverly and David talked on a Sunday night after the children had gone to bed, speaking about the Bombay apartment they would move to, right on the sea, his predecessor's place. "It's ideal," said David, sounding melancholy.

"I'm not going to Bombay," said Beverly. "I'm sorry. I'm *sorry.* I can't."

Shocked, David asked why.

Beverly looked straight ahead, not turning toward him. She

spoke steadily, monotonously, as if she were reading from cue cards. "I'm in love," she said. "Eloise and I love each other and we're going to live together. Eloise knows another couple where the wife left . . . We can live right here, in this apartment. The children are used to the place. Eloise works at the hospital. I'll find part-time work. There'll be the child support . . ."

This announcement, David understood, had required thought and rehearsal. Busy telephones and strange essential absences explained themselves. He looked closely at Beverly and realized that he had not seen her for months. Her hair straggled loose, and the gray had begun to show. She had stopped going to the beauty parlor, David saw, and he had not noticed. He felt angry. "How can you do this to me and the kids! A woman . . ." Then again, as when Alma had ended the affair, he felt relief.

"I know about you and Alma Trust," said Beverly. "Everybody knows." She returned to her speech. "I'll take the children. Eloise loves them. Eloise says that two mothers are better than one. Regina and William will be just fine. You can't take them to Bombay, not by yourself." It was true, David knew — and felt guilty to accept the loss of his children. "They can fly to see you next summer and you can see them in Washington when you're on home leave. OK?"

Alma did not keep promises. When David moved from the apartment to a hotel, shortly before his departure, Alma telephoned and said she needed to see him. Trust Alma, he thought. He opened the door of his hotel room without kissing her. After an argument, in which David's reluctance mixed with curiosity and the old obsession, they took each other's clothes off. They made love, David noted, with rancor and with little comfort. When they finished David told Alma that she had fucked him only because she needed to cuckold her new lover, Piers. She laughed. "Is this the man whose wife leaves him for another woman? Will you sue for alienation of affection? Piers is *not* my lover." Alma found a Gideon in a drawer beside the bed. As she turned the pages, stopping to glance at passages, she looked happily at David. "Do you remember that time I met my old roommate Nicole at National, and hurt your feelings?"

"Yes," said David. "Of course."

"It was Max," Alma said, but David knew that she knew that he knew that she was probably lying.

The night before he flew to Bombay, David woke to find Alma standing beside his bed. "You never lock your door," she said. "I took the babysitter home. We have to be quick." When she had concluded herself, she left.

Widowers' Woods

Mr. Thomas swayed in the back seat of the taxi as it turned into the cemetery through the white wooden gate. The driver slowed down, nearly stopping; when he had checked his closeness to the gate outside his window, he pulled ahead onto a gravel path. Mr. Thomas's vision behind his thick glasses was blurred, leaving only a tiny slip of clarity in the center. In the clear patch, he saw twin tire tracks leading to the summerhouse. The cab charged up to it and braked, scattering cinders. Mr. Thomas heaved forward, bracing his hand against the seat cover to keep from falling. Charlie drove too fast. The lane was built for buggies.

The driver turned around and smiled at him. "Here y'are," he said.

"You drive too fast. There are too many cars on the road," said Mr. Thomas.

"Here y'are," said the driver.

Mr. Thomas used his hands to help move his legs toward the door, which the driver leaned over to open for him. Mr. Thomas swiveled on the plastic cover and let his feet slide to the patchy cinders. When he felt steady, he leaned back inside the car and took out a long cylinder, full of green liquid, that ended in a sharp point. He propped the cylinder against the rail of the summer-house and walked slowly around the taxi to the driver.

"Thank you, Charlie," he said. He took four quarters from his pocket and handed them to the driver.

"Name is Tony, Mr. Thomas. Charlie's dead. See you in an hour, right?" The driver smiled again. Mr. Thomas watched him go from the keyhole of his sight.

It was hot. Mr. Thomas's mouth hung open. He walked into the green summerhouse and sat in the shade, fixing his vision on the pump and the rusty watering can in front of him. Where should he start today? Last week, he had stopped at JAMES HARTWELL 1812–1884. Soon it would be Hettie again. He walked to the door. His fingers felt the roughness of the railing, and when he looked he saw that the paint was peeling away. His vision played like the beam of a flashlight over the flaking paint of the wooden ceiling. Then he stepped through the door and saw that the outside paint was worse. Everywhere the wood was showing through, a dark brown fungus spreading over the summerhouse, reaching out its creepers. It was late October. The weeds had turned brown and died, leaving bare patches of dirt where you raked the leaves. He remembered that he had mentioned the paint to the caretaker. Many times.

He picked up the green cylinder where it lay against the railing and walked into the graveyard. A breeze from the lake across the road came feeling through the heat. Mr. Thomas sensed beneath his shoes that part of the grass was cut and part was not. He straightened and swept his eyes in a circle until he saw the power mower, a bare-chested man behind it. The man waved and shouted, but Mr. Thomas did not hear him or the rasp of the mower. What was his name, the one who did not wear a shirt? Dino.

He passed the Hartwells and paused to read WILLIAM SCRUBBS AND MARY HIS WIFE. Moss made the dates hard to read. Mr. Thomas leaned on his green stick and rested. His vision moved to the street beyond the cemetery and the stores of glass and tile. He heard a noise and turned around. "Hi, Mr. Thomas," shouted the fat bare chest. "Dino. How you doing?" Dino smiled widely in his sweat.

"Crabgrass," said Mr. Thomas.

"You keep it in line," Dino shouted. "You got that thing." He pointed at the green stick. "That's a good thing."

"It's not enough," said Mr. Thomas. He began to feel despair again; Charlie would be back and he had not begun. He bent to the ground and found what he was looking for, the wide, scratchy, gray-green blades, spreading through the real grass that was frail and so easy to kill. He jabbed the point of his green cylinder into the center of the broad leaves and squeezed the bulb at the top.

"Well, so long, Mr. Thomas," said Dino, and rolled away, hitching his trousers over his stomach.

Mr. Thomas moved slowly, searching with the slot of his vision, finding the leaves, plunging and killing. Every minute he stood up and breathed carefully for a while, searching out a breeze to cool himself. Then he bent again and continued his work. The power mower came close to him, receded, and returned again. He smiled and a march tune went through his head. But there were so many. He was still at the Scrubbses'. He looked ahead. After them the Bullmers', and then Hettie's single stone.

He heard noises, and there were children running through the cemetery, so many that they were like beetles scurrying in the grass. They had climbed over the fence in some war of blocks, and they were firing cap pistols at each other. He thought of the Fourth of July. His Uncle Harry's fife and drum corps, Victors of Vicksburg, had marched all day, full of cider. Boys threw fire-crackers all day. Politicians talked, they denounced the empires, the British empire spreading over the world. But then it stopped: An Italian threw a firecracker into an old lady's firecracker stand; she died, and the state passed a law forbidding fireworks. The children defending the summerhouse, banging their guns, have black hair and dark faces. They spread everywhere like weeds.

Mr. Thomas left the Scrubbses' plot and walked past the Bullmers' to Hettie's grave. He felt tired. Scanning Hettie's and his own grass, the swift shuttle of his vision revealed a crop of crabgrass larger than he had ever seen. Though a man fought it all his life, he could not win. It grew over everything; and when he stopped fighting it, it grew over him. He stabbed with his weed killer, jabbing so violently that he missed the roots he aimed for. Everywhere crabgrass spread its claws, the broad hated leaves. He swung at them with his stick, shouting at them, and tears rolled down his cheeks. Then he was so tired and hot that he had to lie down. He got down on his knees and his forearms and stretched out flat. Blades of crabgrass outlined his shape.

He opened his eyes to look into the heart of a weed: In the center of each plant he saw a dark grove of trees; if he could get inside, there would be shade.

An old man in a farmhouse on the side of a hill in New Hamp-shire had been awake for hours. Ben had thought about the flavor checkerberry, about a baseball game between Andover and Wilmot in 1894, about his brother Willard who had died of influenza at the end of the war, and about holes in fences. He lay for a long time remembering a quarrel with his father, which ended with his father telling him stories about the family. Now the sun had risen over the shed, which meant, because it was September, that it was time to get up. What were his chores today?

He dressed quickly, long underwear and overalls and a brown shirt, thick brown socks and old black fancy shoes. In the kitchen the stove was cold; Ben struck a match and lit the oil ring that was set into the place where he had burned wood for fifty years. Slim pipes carried oil from a tank in the woodshed. The fire bloomed toward his hand; he set a kettle over the flame and spooned some Nescafé into a pink cup.

In the garden outside the kitchen window, which Nancy had tended herself, long-legged snapdragons angled toward the sun, horny flowers crumbled with the frost of the night before last. On the lawn a rabbit skittered through tall grass; he thought of his gun. The sound of boiling turned him around. He drank the black coffee quickly and felt the heat uncoil down his arms and legs. He flexed fingers and toes: Time to be doing. What chores? He remembered going to bed tired and listing the chores for tomorrow.

When he was through with his cornflakes, he washed the empty dishes and left them to dry in the rack. The news. He turned on the radio and sat in a rocking chair under the empty canary cage, listening to news and weather. They pulled the boy out of that well. Flowered oilcloth covered the table in front of him; at the corners of the table the shiny surface had split and fibers showed through. He liked to rub his hand against the fibers. Above the table was a calendar, the month of August with a picture of field corn tall in the sun. He rocked back and forth. The weather was fair, Eastport to Block Island.

He put on a cloth cap and a suit coat and walked to the barn. Ghost cows turned to look at him as he walked in the empty tie-up. In a corner, where whitewash turned gray on spider webs, his milking stool hung next to his pail; for a few seconds he milked the herd and cooled the milk. He looked out the back window, where the necks of twenty horses had worn the sill smooth, at the dry bed of a stream, and at weeds turning gray with September frost.

On the main floor, old boards were still wispy with hay; clusters of harness hung from wooden pegs; ladders he had made himself led up to the first loft and from there to the second. He put his hand on the silky polished wood of a rung. Everything turned smoother, though he remembered slivers when the ladders were new. Birds flew in and out over his head.

There were lumps of hay, nearly black now, under the eaves of the barn. Hay reminded him of a chore: He walked down the hill to the shed where he kept the hayrack and looked at the side with the missing spoke. In the woodshed he bent among ash sticks and picked one that he took back to the hayrack; he measured it against the gap; he drew a line on it with a pencil he found in his overalls. He was pleased to find it there. Then he sat on an overturned sap bucket and whittled and smoothed the new spoke. His mind mumbled over stories, friends, smiling and shaking hands and eating fresh ice cream from a dish outdoors under a maple tree. When he was finished, he fitted the new spoke in place on the rack.

Back in the kitchen he hung up his cap and suit coat and lit the oil ring again. He rubbed his hands together above the flame and set the kettle over it. He opened the refrigerator and took out a plate of lunchmeat: fourth day from that can. He sliced off a thick piece and put it on a clean plate, adding a handful of potato chips from a cellophane bag. Water boiled for his coffee; he sat at the set-tubs on a tall stool and ate lunch.

Then he washed and lay on the sofa in the sitting room where the air never moved. Because he had not yet started burning ash in the big square stove, he pulled a quilt over himself. For a minute he kept his eyes open, looking at the tall radio standing on its legs, at the glassed-in bookcase stuffed with books and photographs, at the long table clock that never worked properly, and at the picture of Franconia Notch. What chore would occupy the afternoon? Then he slept lightly.

When he woke the sun shone into the parlor past the trailing ivy that Nancy had put in the window. He stood and looked out at the hayfields, big stone and mountain beyond. Hay waved, tall and gray-brown. Winter and snow would trample it down, and new grass would tangle with it next spring. A good hay day.

He clapped his hands together suddenly, making a noise like a rifle in the still room. He looked at the pictures on top of the piano and said out loud, "I'm going fencing." At least, he would take a look at the pasture fence. He was happy and he hummed a hymn tune: "I walked in the garden alone." It was a good day for walking in the pasture, sun and a light wind.

He put on his cap and jacket and walked up the road. Ahead of him was the big stone, a single boulder the size of a woodshed, where—someone told him when he was a boy—the Indians had met for their powwows. As he went past it, he paused to touch the stone arrow in the side, a strange indentation shaped like an arrow, as clean and accurate as if it had been chiseled. He ran his forefinger from the point of the arrow around the whole shape of it, up the narrow stem, and into the wavy feather at the end.

He stepped through a gate in the fieldstone wall; the poles were out of their stone notches, lying on the ground. No need to set them back. He walked inside his wall as it turned a right angle and headed uphill. Then the wall turned into a fence of wire and felled branches, with holes where the wire had rusted through or a branch had rotted. He made a point of remembering the broken places.

As he walked more deeply into the old pasture, new pine grew tightly around him, and cowflops on the path next to the fence were gray and fragile with age. The pine made him think of coffins, but under his feet he felt the ridges of old plowing. He had come to the potato place, as he had learned to call it when he was a boy, where his grandfather had cleared timber and planted potatoes, way back in the thirties before the Mexican War.

The fence disappeared entirely; pines grew smaller until they were gone. He climbed a rise and saw the bowl of a high valley before him, a smaller saucer of fertile land green with potato plants. At the far side three men and a boy were working, grabbing in clods with long-handled claws for potatoes. When they had dug up a hill they bent and gathered potatoes into the burlap sack each one carried with him. He walked across the harvested rows to join them. Anyone can use another hand. A man with a black beard leaned on his fork: "Will you give us a hand?"

He took over the tool that the boy had held. He dug a row of hills. Now the boy went row to row, cropping potatoes into sacks.

The men did not have to stoop and gather potatoes, and the rows moved faster. He dug easily and slowly in the loose soil, tossing aside the green plants with their brown, frostbitten edges. The muscles in his back grew tired, but he felt good. The sun lowered. A woman walked toward them along the edge of the field, coming from the direction of the farm. She carried a white enamel coffeepot and a wicker basket. They sat under a sugar maple and drank hot coffee, milk and sugar already mixed in it, and each ate a hard-boiled egg and a piece of custard pie. The bearded man and his son sat with the woman, apart from the two hands, who ate steadily and silently. The bearded man asked him, "Will you stay to harvest?"

It was late; his back ached; he felt happily tired. "I'm going back," he said. "I'm obliged for the coffee and the pie."

He left them while they finished their coffee under the maple; he walked back the way he had come. A bear crashed past him in the underbrush, not seeing him. First time he'd seen a bear since he was a boy. The trees were huge and old; it was colder; he'd better light the stove in the sitting room. Though he was sure he was near it, he could not find the fence. When he came to the flat part where the road was, he could not find the road. He felt his way in the direction of the house and came into a clearing where the big stone, as huge as a barn in the twilight, gathered the darkness of the forest. The side where he felt for the stone arrow was smooth.

Further, he found himself on a flat nook of land he recognized, but there was a grove of rock maple on it—great trees three hundred years old, trunks as hard as granite. He admired the broad, tough leaves, which were brilliant orange and red, and delicate yellow. He was lost, yet a comfortable laziness came over him. He stood on the matted leaves, in the middle of his sitting room, and after a while sat down and leaned back against a tree.

When Mr. Thomas found his way into the woods, the harsh light retreated; he felt cool and strong. He walked on matted leaves, not caring about the animals; he passed a huge boulder. Then he saw that the woods were full of old men, sleeping or sitting quietly by themselves. Widowers' Woods, he thought, that's what they ought to call it.

Argument and Persuasion

I

A HUSBAND AND WIFE named Raoul and Marie lived in a house beside a river next to a forest. One afternoon Raoul told Marie that he had to travel to Paris overnight on business. As soon as he left, Marie paid the Ferryman one franc to row her across the river to the house of her lover, Pierre. Marie and Pierre made love all night. Just before dawn, Marie dressed to go home, to be sure that she arrived before Raoul returned. When she reached the Ferryman, she discovered that she had neglected to bring a second franc for her return journey. She asked the Ferryman to trust her; she would pay him back. He refused: A rule is a rule, he said.

If she walked north by the river she could cross it on a bridge, but between the bridge and her house a Murderer lived in the forest and killed anybody who entered. So Marie returned to Pierre's house to wake him and borrow a franc. She found the door locked; she banged on it; she shouted as loudly as she could; she threw pebbles against Pierre's bedroom windows. Pierre awoke hearing her but he was tired and did not want to get out of bed. Women, he thought, once you give in, they take advantage of you. Pierre went back to sleep.

Marie returned to the Ferryman. She would give him *ten* francs by midmorning. He refused to break the rules of his job; they told him cash only; he did what they told him. Marie returned to Pierre, with the same lack of result, as the sun started to rise.

Desperate, she ran north along the riverbank, crossed the bridge, and entered the Murderer's forest.

2

At nine A.M. on a cool April morning, seventeen young women sat in plastic classroom chairs, each with a paddle-shaped writing surface. When Dr. Silva finished telling the story, he paused until the girls stopped their note-taking and looked up at him. He smiled as he had smiled in a hundred other composition classes when he had told about Raoul and Marie. He continued: "This is not a trick story. There is no correct answer, but for forty minutes, please argue an answer to this question: Which of the characters in the story is morally most responsible for Marie's death?"

He wrote the question on the board and turned back to the class. "This impromptu gives you the opportunity to shape an argument. Be logical. In the next five minutes you may ask questions. There will be no further questions after five minutes are up. Do your thinking now." Myra Bobnick was already writing. "Do not start writing your impromptu before you have thought it out." Myra raced into her second page as if there were a contest for the most pages. Helen DeVane looked as puzzled as ever and put her hand up. "I will list and spell all names on the blackboard," Dr. Silva said. He wrote:

RAOUL

MARIE

FERRYMAN

PIERRE

MURDERER

When he finished, he nodded in Helen's direction.

"Did like this really happen?"

He could never tell what Helen's question would be, but he knew it would be dull-witted. He also knew that she didn't really want an answer; she wanted only to postpone the moment of writing. When he answered Helen, he feared that he sounded so patient that he revealed his annoyance. "It doesn't matter, Helen. Certainly; why not? But it's just a story, something to write about." She nodded her head, but the puzzlement never left her face.

Young women crossed their blue-jeaned legs and addressed the lined pads before them. This class was the first of his three classes on Wednesday. All would do the same impromptu, and if some of the later classes heard the story ahead of time, he knew it would make no difference. The girls chewed their fingernails or their Bics, either thinking or trying to look as if they were thinking. Magda had a question. "The ferry guy, did he work for himself, I mean with his own boat?"

"In the story," said Dr. Silva, "he implies that somebody else makes the rules."

There were no more questions. Now he could daydream for half an hour. He enjoyed this moment of English Composition 101, when fifteen or twenty pens scratched in front of him and he could look out the window at the grosbeaks coming to the feeder he had put there. Young female heads bent over paper like so many birds poking for sunflower seed. He checked his class list. There would have been eighteen but Jeanette was still in the infirmary. A year ago they had been graduating seniors in their suburban high schools; now they were freshmen at Connecticut Hills, a two-year college once called a finishing school, where he knew himself fortunate to have a job. He did not write books; for the good jobs you had to write books. Most of his work was three or four sections of English Composition — teaching the art of English prose to girls who could not, most of them, read anything more complicated than the labels of their cashmere sweaters. One term a year he relaxed into a section of the sophomore Introduction to Great Books, a soft reward for all his labor over comma splices: *The Odyssey,* a touch of Thucydides, *Othello.*

Mary Ellen Budd was walking up to the desk. He shook his head; no questions after five minutes. Mary Ellen looked hopeless, sat down, and wrote nothing for the next ten minutes. He understood: She was demonstrating Dr. Silva's injustice; he also understood that she would get over it.

He could not remember who had told him the story of Raoul and Marie. It was early in graduate school, those happy-go-lucky first three years of marriage and provisional adulthood, in-between time that was also the best time, he often acknowledged, though not out loud; Anne did enough acknowledging out loud, when she had had something to drink. Back then in Ann Arbor someone at a party had told the story; it was supposed to be an anecdote Camus liked to tell, asking, "Who's most to blame?" Arthur Silva had said from the start that he knew the answer even if there wasn't supposed to be one: the Murderer. It made him feel morally clear-sighted to give this answer and defend it.

He looked at the pretty heads bent down before him: children of privilege, growing up rich in America, no brains. And when they had brains, which happened at Connecticut Hills more often than you might expect, the brains were well trained to believe that they were stupid, or to know by an unstated rule that if they wished to remain daughters who were loved, cherished, and protected, they had better *act* stupid.

Bethany had finished her page and a half and checked it over: obedient girl, and not stupid by half. It was Dr. Silva's task, as he saw it, to teach girls like Bethany Trager not to write sentences, not to employ the major rhetorical patterns, not to write A themes, but: *I am not dumb.* This was his mission at Connecticut Hills, and when he succeeded it was gratifying. He sighed, reminding himself that it was opposite to the lesson that he had learned. After five years in the Ph.D. program at the University of Michigan, with the M.A. behind him and generals twice failed, he had been summoned by the Graduate Faculty Committee and requested to withdraw from the Ph.D. program. Of course they would help him get a job, they assured him, for he was a competent teacher of composition. They apologized that their judgment had failed when they admitted him to the program, but they could not therefore compound the error by permitting him to continue. After he pleaded his case, the textual scholar Waldo Slaughter silenced him with one sentence: "You are not Ph.D.

material." The words remained permanently attached to him, as if they were printed on his forehead in diploma script. He remembered how old Braithewaite kept nodding his head, as if with encouragement, at every devastating judgment.

Oh, to take those words home to Anne, with Joanie only two years old! — Anne who had quit the M.A. program in French to take a job when they married, then quit her job to have Joanie. As it happened, the promised support consisted of a one-year job at a day school in Flint. After which, with a certain amount of back-door help from the guiltier senior professors, Arthur Silva had been accepted into the doctoral program of the education department of an old normal school turned state university, and in two years he wore the desired letters after his name.

"Time's up!" he said. "You have an extra minute for checking." Five hours later — two more classes, brown-bag lunch, office hours — he bicycled home with fifty-seven impromptus about a murder in a forest in generalized France.

3

When Raoul returned from Paris at noon he was exhausted and hungry. It annoyed him that Marie was nowhere about. It was unlike her, although she sometimes took a *fin* in the morning with one of her gabby old-wife friends. There was of course her ridiculous *affaire de coeur* with Pierre, about which Raoul pretended convenient ignorance. They had, after all, been married a dozen years. And after all, what was he doing in Paris? He sighed in delicious recollection of a seamstress.

Raoul was too tired to make the rounds of the cafés. He

swallowed some stale bread with sweet butter and a slab of cold pink lamb. He read three pages in *L'Encyclopédie* and slept until seven o'clock in the evening. He woke and called Marie's name, intent on complaining about her absence. When she did not answer he was suddenly frightened. Where in hell was Marie?

4

Thursday was Dr. Silva's day without classes; therefore he let Wednesday be theme day and spent all Thursday at the breakfast table, blitzing through a stack of papers with his red pencil and his *Harbrace College Handbook*—a dreadful text, but he knew the symbols for correction so well that they appeared as characters in his dreams. When you had sixty themes on the same subject—Dr. Silva had worked at schools where he taught composition to a hundred students a term—the first twenty went quickly. You began with one or two of the best, to set a measure. You knew who the best would be. After one class meeting, you knew which students would have A's at the end of the term. This knowledge depressed him—what was the purpose of teaching?—but he used this knowledge. You set the rest against the models, almost like grading on a curve. With a free theme it was harder, but he rarely gave free themes anymore. The students complained that they had no ideas; freedom was the last thing they wanted: They wanted to know what he wanted so that they could do what he wanted so that they could receive the C's that they wanted.

Anne brought him a pot of coffee in a thermal jug before she went to work in the travel agency. Familiar sarcasms dropped sleepily from the corner of her mouth. Now that Joanie had finished college and worked in San Francisco, they could survive without Anne's job, and usually her jobs didn't last very long. Usually she was fired for being unpleasant to customers. What people called sarcasm he knew for disappointment. He knew who had let her down, and that was why, as he told himself, he never answered her bitterness with bitterness. Every now and then she was fired for drinking, and if she were home all day — Dr. Silva's teaching schedule was long, with conferences, office hours, and the writing lab on Mondays and Fridays — what would she do with her time but drink? She was holding on to her present job, although her complaints accelerated. One day she would leave work early; one day he would bicycle home to find her sitting with a bottle.

On this Thursday he was more than halfway through by the time Anne came home for lunch. But the remaining themes always took half again as long, and sometimes he put the last papers off until the next morning, working from six to eight before the nine o'clock class that began his long Friday.

"What's the score?" Anne said as she came in.

"About like last year," he said. He looked at the sheet where he kept tab, four upright marks slanted through to make five. "Marie twenty, Pierre five, Raoul four, Ferryman one."

5

Pierre woke in his house across the river about the time Raoul returned from Paris. The cook who doubled as serving maid brought him brioches and café au lait while he read *Le Monde*.

For a long time Pierre felt slightly ill at ease, as if there were something he had forgotten to do. Twice he checked his calendar, but there was nothing on until teatime. He adjusted his foulard in the mirror and drank more coffee. Then he remembered: That slut Marie had knocked on his door all night! He filled with indignation for the sake of his friend Raoul. Perhaps it was time to give Marie her walking papers, amusing as she had seemed at the beginning. Pierre curled his lip. Pierre sharpened the points of his black mustache.

He allowed himself to think of potential replacements. Perhaps it was time to allow Marguerite the pleasures of his bed. She seemed ready a month ago, and surely Alphonse would be complaisant if not downright grateful. On the other hand there was Sylvie, a touch young perhaps at fifteen, but therefore perhaps entertaining. At any rate, he felt certain, there would soon be an opening. These ruminations relieved him of his annoyance and cheered him up. He allowed *la petite bonne*, who was a great-grandmother at forty-seven, to leave when she had cleaned up after lunch, although Rose-Rose was not due until four o'clock.

6

After lunch Arthur Silva worked until three forty-five, when he had to interrupt his day at home. He stood, stretched, unlocked his bike, and pumped toward the campus for a special conference with Jeanette, who had been ill for two weeks and required makeup assignments. He enjoyed the break in his day of correcting impromptus, but as he pedaled he could not clear them from his mind. Marie kept getting most of the votes: She should have done this, she should have done that; she was at fault because she forgot to bring return fare for the Ferryman, because of her taste in rotten Pierre, because she knew that the Murderer was in the forest—and always, implicit if unmentioned, because she was an unfaithful wife.

Tomorrow he would arch his eyebrows and ask Myra Bobnick if she really felt that infidelity was a capital offense. In his ten o'clock, he would ask Ginger Hagstrom about the idea behind her conclusion: "Marie was begging for it." He was not sure that he would raise Mary Ellen Budd's argument in class. It had surprised him a little, for Mary Ellen was only quietly attractive— not heavily made up, not tightly jeaned—and she had poured scorn upon Marie for her stupidity in not lying her way out of her predicament. Marie was morally responsible for her own death, according to Mary Ellen, because she was so dumb—because after daylight she could have borrowed a franc from practically anybody on Pierre's side of the river, and if Raoul was already back by the time the Ferryman rowed her across, she would just tell him that she had felt like taking a walk after a restless night. Professor Silva sighed for Mary Ellen and for her husbands and lovers; then he sighed for himself and everybody else.

No more lies, thank goodness. Most of the lies happened while Joanie was still little, when he and Anne lurched more than once toward the cliffs of divorce. There had been a long period of calm before Anne's last fling, four years ago at St. Hilda's. And even earlier, he reminded himself, there had been stretches of good time when they had been loyal and kind to each other. He remembered with gratitude the first year of his graduate work at

State, when they had joined the Presbyterian church so that Joanie could go to Sunday school, and to their surprise followed their minister in his clear love of Jesus, whose figure clarified momentarily for both of them and allowed them notions of compassion and grace. But every good memory slid into something bad. That idyll ended when Anne discovered the letters a student of nursing had written Arthur. He could not for the life of him remember how he had allowed himself to ruin their calm by drifting into a casual affair. He remembered only feeling powerless, fated, carried like a chip on the stream.

Deliberately he turned his mind back to the present. Maybe he could write a paper for *College English* about this assignment. He had often thought about it; he had made some notes. He used this impromptu every term when he introduced the subject of Argumentation. It revealed unstated hypotheses, unacknowledged and unexamined; it revealed Logical Fallacies.

Every year a few students named Raoul on the grounds of priority. First, he was a bad husband or Marie would not have been unfaithful; second, since leaving her alone was the earliest fault, it was the most grievous. Few students, in all the years, voted for the Ferryman—because he was only following orders, because his motive seemed less passionate. When they did vote for him, it was on the same grounds: Because his motive seemed least important, mercy would have cost him least; therefore his refusal to transport Marie was capricious, which made him morally most responsible. Dr. Silva rather liked this argument, because he remembered (part of the story told in Ann Arbor) that in France the Ferryman always won the vote: Gallic disgust over the small bureaucrat, *le petit fonctionnaire*. The Ferryman had won Anne's vote, years back in Ann Arbor; she thought it was because she had spent her junior year abroad in France.

Students who found Pierre guiltiest usually showed the most illogic — and they were the sweetest students, unsophisticated believers in romantic love. He could imagine how cynical Mary Ellen Budd would be about such arguments: We could use her, during the class meeting, to argue with the illogic of romantic outrage. The question of greater culpability — he would explain after Mary Ellen had made the point unclearly — is not the same as the question of foulness of character. Similarly, of course, he could find another student to rebut Mary Ellen's equation of Marie's moral culpability with Marie's disinclination to lie.

He smiled with fondness as he remembered how Joanie, who was only sixteen when he told her the story, had turned furious at Pierre. It was in the living room of the dormitory apartment at St. Hilda's, while Anne was still sober and faithful and Joanie a devoted daughter, when things for a while went well. He had never known Joanie so outraged, as he gently questioned her premises. But it had turned sour. Anne's sarcasm sent Joanie in a rage to her room, as a few years later it sent her across the continent to San Francisco.

Dr. Silva pushed uphill toward the bicycle rack. Every pleasant memory started a rabbit that, when it found its hole, found stale defeat. He tried remembering how lucky he was in his job at Connecticut Hills, but it made him remember how St. Hilda's was good for two years only; then it became a job he left on his own initiative, because Anne carried on with the famously philandering bursar and humiliated Arthur, showing affection to her lover even in public, even at a Christmas party with students.

That January in his classroom he had found a map rolled down in front of his blackboard and when he zipped it up had read: DR. SILVA IS A WIMP.

But nobody voted for the Murderer. He locked his bike, walking to his office. Once, half a dozen years ago, at St. Hilda's as a matter of fact, a freshman intellectual turned up in his class. Clearly the system had failed. When she advanced her theory that the person who committed the crime was the most responsible for the crime, the class unanimously proclaimed that she was crazy. If you were a murderer, murder was part of the job description, wasn't it?

7

The Ferryman rode his bicycle home at eight A.M. after his twelve-hour stint. The daytime help had showed up on time for once. His wife—fat, ugly, and agreeable—bustled at the stove, flour whitening her arms up to her elbows.

"How'd it go?" she said. "Much work?"

He hung his beret on a peg and slouched to the table, yawning. "Seventeen trips. Seventeen francs. What's for dinner?"

"Oeufs à la Russe, truite au beurre, Châteaubriand (bleu, d'accord), pommes frites, choux de Bruxelles, salade verte, and napoléon. Somebody go just one way?"

With his mouth full of egg and mayonnaise, he took a moment to answer. "That slut with the brown curls who screws around with that fruit on the other side of the river when her husband visits his whore in Paris. Can you beat it? She didn't bring money for the ride back!"

His wife turned the steak in the skillet, stirred the sprouts, and drained the potatoes. "What did she do, try the forest?"

"Hey, how do I know? No skin off my ass. *Tant pis. Merde alors.* People get what's coming to them. When they call your number, your number's up. The bullet's got your name on it, you're dead. The moving finger writes. Rules are rules. I was only following orders."

She served the salad. "You always were a bunghole, honey," she said.

8

Although he was two minutes early, Jeanette was waiting in her baggy jeans and sweatshirt outside his office, looking pale and anxious as she always did.

"Sorry if I'm late," said Dr. Silva. He made a mental note that his feeder was empty outside his classroom next door; he would bring sunflower seed in the morning. When Jeanette sat down and took out her notebook, he asked if she felt able to undertake her makeup work. She nodded, poised with pen and notebook. Dr. Silva read from his class schedule, first the reading assignments, then last week's theme—a three-hundred-word essay using a rhetorical pattern and keyed to a reading assignment. Could she finish this theme in the next ten days? Jeanette nodded.

Then he told her that beginning tomorrow the class hour

would be devoted to Argumentation. He asked her if she could spend forty minutes, tonight, writing something like an impromptu — he smiled as he said he trusted her not to spend more than forty minutes — and bring it to class tomorrow. If she could do the latest thing first, he explained, she would be ready to keep up with the classwork, and she could catch up on the old work as she was able. He was conscious again that he was an easy and generous teacher, as he intended to be.

Jeanette thought she could manage, and Dr. Silva for the nth time in his life told the story of Raoul and Marie. Coming to the part where Marie was refused a second time by the Ferryman, and a second time by Pierre, he hurried because Jeanette turned pale until she looked the color of a rainy day. Before he could finish, she vomited over his desk.

With a secretary's help, and with the help of another student waiting outside another office, Dr. Silva walked Jeanette to the college infirmary, although she whimpered that she did not want to return.

When she was put to bed and sedated he paused by the desk of the head nurse, Mrs. Williams. He asked what Jeanette's illness had been. Mrs. Williams was surprised that he did not know, although they tried to keep such things quiet. After a pause for discretion's sake, she told him: Jeanette had visited a boy's college on a blind date, got drunk, and fraternity boys gang-raped her. She was doing quite well, the nurse told him; the school psychologist was reassuring, although this relapse would trouble him.

Something like this happened every year, Mrs. Williams said, at the same place more often than not. Those fraternities should be abolished! But for all the warnings every autumn —

deans and housemothers and seniors — something like this happened almost *every year*. Mrs. Williams shook her head. Tears filled her eyes. Tears filled Dr. Silva's eyes also; shame started in him. Mrs. Williams pulled herself together and acknowledged that the girls, even those most brutalized, by and large survived. She could mention, but she wouldn't, one or two prominent alumnae who had endured something like Jeanette's humiliation.

Dr. Silva knew that his face was bright red as he returned to his office and with paper towels from the washroom cleaned up vomit. He left the window open six inches and bicycled home. Maybe this would be a good night for going to the movies, he thought. He remembered that there was a western at the shopping mall. He and Anne liked westerns, with their clear, simplified morality. Anne had picked up a taste for them during her year in France, where the Parisian critics were making much of them. But he found her already ironical with her second whiskey, smoking Camel after Camel between yellowed fingers, her grayed hair straggling and her face smudged. Dr. Silva recognized marks of boredom and self-loathing. He poured himself a drink and threw it away. He could not speak to Anne, not now when she had been drinking. His mind kept giving him one excuse: How could he have known? The excuse did not help; when he looked at the papers left to be corrected he felt revulsion. "I guess I'll do them in the morning," he said as if to Anne.

"What else is new?" she said.

All night he was restless with guilty and defensive thoughts. He would no sooner fall asleep than Anne would snore and wake him. He turned her gently onto her side and lay still, awake and miserable. At six o'clock he made a pot of coffee and settled down to correct the last dozen themes mechanically. He wrote in the margins, "Is this a capital offense?" with the same mild irony that he had used yesterday and twenty years earlier.

When Anne woke up at seven-thirty he had finished the papers and made more coffee. His mind wandered while *Good Morning, America* talked about famine in Ethiopia, a plane crash in Russia, Princess Di's pregnancy, an Iranian boat capsizing, the execution of a crazed killer in Florida, a high-pressure zone over the East, and Wayne Gretzky's hat trick. He bicycled to his nine o'clock class trembling and uncertain, as if he were meeting his first class twenty-five years ago.

9

When the nighttime Ferryman went back to work at eight P.M., fresh from breakfast, Raoul and Pierre were waiting for him. Raoul asked questions and the Ferryman answered them defiantly, making the point that rules are rules and he was only following orders. At this last remark Pierre spat in the dust at the Ferryman's feet, then twirled the ends of his mustache. The two men stared at each other. Doubtless Pierre had been less than forthright in recounting his own behavior the previous night, and therefore showed contempt for the Ferryman's petty rigidity. Raoul remained cool as he watched the confrontation.

Then he interrupted. "OK," he said. "She must have gone into the forest. What are we going to do?"

Pierre supplied a solution. "Let's all go to sleep," he said. "She's probably just hanging around somewhere. With a friend.

Have you tried the saloon? If she isn't back by tomorrow, maybe we ought to call the sheriff."

Raoul turned suddenly bitter. "And then some liberal judge will put the Murderer in an insane asylum. I say we raise a posse."

Pierre said he'd drink to that, and the Ferryman jumped up and yodeled. "Well, I'll be hornswoggled," he declared, slapping his ten-gallon hat against his thigh. "Heh, heh, heh," he croaked, banging his friend Pierre on the back. "I reckon we just got ourselves invited to a necktie party!"

10

Dr. Silva waited until the seventeen young female bodies, sleepy in their sweaters at nine o'clock, gathered before him. It was Jeanette's class, and to his relief she was not there. He realized as he waited for quiet that all the young women in his classes had known about Jeanette's assault from the day it happened. When he had told the story day before yesterday, what could they have thought?

They watched him take the rubber band off the papers and quieted down, looking up at him expectantly.

"It was Marie, wasn't it?" said Helen DeVane, followed by a small cheer from most of the class.

"Now I told you that there was no correct answer," he said, "but, yes, you agreed as a class that Marie's moral responsibility was the greatest." He read from his tally sheet for the nine A.M. class: "Marie fourteen, Raoul two, Pierre one."

Girls applauded. It was the game side of this assignment

that made it effective. Today it disturbed him, and he spoke almost as if he were cross: "But the point is your arguments. Remember, we are studying Argumentation. I am sure that you all spent last night rereading chapter eight of *Writing Well*, 'Argument and Persuasion.' Magda, tell us why Marie was the most responsible."

Magda put down an unlit cigarette. "Because she cheated on her husband is why. I mean, if she hadn't cheated, it would never have happened?"

Bethany Trager was pumping her arm. He nodded in her direction. "But if her husband hadn't gone off and left her, it wouldn't have like happened in the first place, or if the ferryboat guy had trusted her. I say Raoul, because he *started* it by going away, because he was like the *first*."

Deriding voices defended Raoul from the charge, and said the Ferryman had the *least* to do with it . . . Dr. Silva heard a voice proclaiming Pierre. "Pearl?" he said.

"Yeah," she said, "Pierre did it, I mean he's the worst, you know? I mean there they are, you know, doing it all night and he won't even open the door for her when she's screaming and crying? What a rat."

At this point the class erupted with laughter and argument. It always happened so—and this year he did not want it to happen. He let them shout, out of control, as the Marie majority poured scorn on the rest. Then he waved his hands for silence. In desperation he tried playing the old tape: "Helen," he said, "you said Marie was guilty for her own death because she had committed adultery. Does anyone find anything to criticize in Helen's logic?" No one spoke.

"You all know what logic is; you all read the chapter." More silence. "Helen, do you think that adultery should be punished?"

Helen lit a cigarette and looked as if she felt picked on.

Dr. Silva continued: "Do you think adultery should be punished by death?" Looking out the window, he realized that he had forgotten to bring sunflower seed.

After a sullen moment Barbie Hawkes put up her hand. Dr. Silva nodded, feeling his stomach tremble. "But, I know," she said, "but she really was like asking for it, you've got to admit, right?" Dr. Silva's nausea rose as he watched the girls in front of him nod their heads in sage agreement. "She was a dope," somebody said, and through the noise of general agreement he heard Mary Ellen laughing as she described the ways in which Marie could have lied her way out. Somebody's voice, louder than the rest, summed it all up: "She got what was coming to her." Dr. Silva stared at the floor, no longer listening. The class quieted, as if the students felt that they had assumed an authority that wasn't theirs. Silence forced Dr. Silva to speak.

"I wonder," he said, "if any of you gave thought to the notion that the guiltiest person might be the Murderer."

When in earlier years he had made this suggestion, his class usually erupted into a hubbub of derision that he gradually tamed by argument. This time, when he spoke, he caused no hubbub. Someone said "Awww," but the sentiment drifted away unconfirmed. As he looked from face to face, the girls lowered their eyes. They were embarrassed, and at first he did not know why. Then Bethany Trager took pity. "I thought about him," she said, "but then I decided: If he's just a Murderer, if that's all he is, then he must be like crazy, and if you're crazy, how can you be guilty?"

Dr. Silva spoke gently, reaching back to old words because

he didn't know how to speak new ones. "You're making an assumption," he said. "The story doesn't say the Murderer is crazy. The story says someone murders people who come through the woods. Haven't we convicted and executed people who did that? Multiple murderers? Haven't we called them guilty? If murdering is crazy, then by your logic are all murderers innocent?"

There might be a number of answers to that one, he knew; of course, as he often said to Anne after he had stated a conviction, he didn't mean that he was right . . . He felt his face grow red; he felt his heart pound; he did not want to speak the old words. "You made another assumption," he said. "You said that you 'thought about him.' Do you see why that's an assumption?"

Bethany shook her head. Dr. Silva went on, "How do you know that the Murderer is a man?"

Bethany's face showed a quick glint of intelligence. At the same time, Dr. Silva became aware of a sound from the rest of the room like air escaping from a tire, a collective sigh that expressed mild boredom and mild disgust. He looked at the faces — Mary Ellen, Magda, Pearl, Barbie, Helen, Joan, Tracy, Stacy, Myra, Susan, Kimberly, Hulda, Bethany . . . Pretty faces, most of them, parentally cherished faces of young American women. Mostly they looked at him, he realized, with contempt — or if it was not so strong as contempt, it was condescension: *Dr. Silva is a wimp.* They knew what men do and what women do to outwit or evade what men do. They were sorry for him or contemptuous of him because he did not know.

Suddenly he heard himself plead: "*Please* don't accept this! You don't have to accept this! You think it's all right that Marie got murdered. You think it's *natural.* Why do you think you have to put up with this? Why don't you . . . ?"

He stopped short of mentioning Jeanette, and he did not know what to say next. He did not know what they should do.

11

As soon as Marie entered the forest she heard footsteps behind her. When she reached the clearing she turned around quickly to face him. He showed no hesitation but emerged from the underbrush to face her in the grassy opening gradually lightening with dawn. He was dressed like a clerk from the Second Empire, or like the emperor himself, with a derby set squarely on his head, a small mustache, and a pince-nez that made his eyes look narrow. He wore clean gray gloves and carried an umbrella.

MARIE: I take it that you are the Murderer.

MURDERER: I take it that you are my next victim, since you have voluntarily entered the forest that is my domain.

MARIE: If you wish it, I shall be your next victim. I do, however, question your use of the word "voluntarily," or the idea implicit in the word.

MURDERER: You are well-spoken.

MARIE: I enter the forest not voluntarily but under compulsion because of the action, inaction, and potential action of three men. You are the fourth man.

MURDERER: In your opinion, is the compulsion singular or plural? I speak of course in metaphor. Are we four men, one man, or all men?

MARIE: Speaking historically, you are one man. But one or many, your violence is not requisite. It is within the power of your will to commit not murder but mercy.

MURDERER: For what reason would I spare your life when I have spared no one else's?

MARIE: By sparing my life you proclaim your freedom. Are you an automaton, able only to perform according to rote?

MURDERER: And if I spared you, how would it affect my reputation? It would be taken as a sign of weakness. Your fear recognizes my power, which neighborhood anxiety confirms.

MARIE: On the contrary, mercy would prove your power and your strength. What power resides in the predictable?

MURDERER: A deal of power resides in the predictable — unless and until power shows itself mutable, capricious, whimsical. Invariable obligation, not to say routine, sustains my omnipotence.

MARIE: And in your inflexibility you make danger for yourself. If you showed mercy on occasion, your neighbors could allow themselves hope in connection with your power and your forest.

MURDERER: A moderate acquaintance with human history makes evident: *Power's use is ineluctable.* Allow me to ask: From what does my power derive?

MARIE: From physical strength.

MURDERER: From what do your concepts of pity and compassion derive?

MARIE: From my physical weakness, or from slave morality, if you will; you are indebted to the insane philosopher Nietzsche. Jesus had a number of things to say about weakness and strength.

MURDERER: Jesus, I need hardly inform you, bred no progeny. Remarkable indeed for moral suggestions and personal behavior, he did not disturb the characteristics of the double helix. Although we may differ on the etiology of ethics, you will agree that ideas are acquired characteristics that do not alter the gene pool.

MARIE: The dove descended.

MURDERER: And quickened one womb. In order to rid the woods of murderers, the Holy Ghost—possibly in the form of gene-altering radiation—must descend with regularity, must perhaps quicken every womb for three generations. I kill you for the reason that you understand, that you even accept: I am stronger than you are.

MARIE: It is my part to tell you: When you kill me because you are stronger than I am, the politics of this murder is only incidentally sexual, or I should say physiological—an incidence, naturally enough, that I find poignant—for you authorize your own murder, on the same principle of strength, as soon as a younger or more muscular or more determined Murderer enters the woods. Or a lynch mob, which is your body multiplied by other bodies both weak and strong.

MURDERER: Well understood. Are we ready, can-be, for to begin?

12

Dr. Silva canceled his classes and bicycled back to the apartment. He lay on the bed with his head whirling, nauseated when he closed his eyes, desperately tired when he kept them open. After a while he heard Anne come home for lunch, fix a tuna fish sandwich, watch part of a game show, and return to work. With the shades still drawn in the bedroom he lay on his back looking at the ceiling without making a sound until she was gone. Then he rose and paced, bedroom through living room to kitchen and back again. On one of his passes he chewed a rib of celery; later he ate a handful of bologna and heated bitter coffee.

By the time Anne returned at five-thirty he had made a decision. On Monday, he said, he would submit his resignation to the dean of Connecticut Hills. Over the weekend he would update his curriculum vitae and draft a letter seeking employment. By the end of next week he would have written every community college in California, maybe four-year schools as well — but California's community colleges were famous. Wherever they wound up, he said while Anne nodded, they would be closer to Joanie.

Anne drank Dubonnet slowly while Arthur daydreamed aloud, growing more enthusiastic as his plans turned more concrete. When he paused Anne was agreeable: They should see the country before they got too old; maybe after a few years in California they could take early retirement; maybe they should think again about a trailer in Arizona; maybe she should return to school; maybe she should go into social work, as she had often thought.

By the time they went to bed that evening, Dr. Silva had almost forgotten his shame. Then he remembered: He would have to find a new way to introduce Argument and Persuasion. He had the notion again, which he usually dismissed quickly: Maybe it was time to leave teaching. But what could he do instead? He smiled sleepily, thinking, I could be rich. When he was a child he had wanted a car as long as a Pullman. He dove toward sleep remembering a Pierce-Arrow that parked on Thursdays when he was a small boy in front of his father's grocery. The chauffeur teased him gently while the old lady went inside to feel the vegetables. His mother told him that he could not be a chauffeur because he was not black. When he said that then he wanted to be a widow, because he knew that Archibald's boss was a widow, his mother repeated his remark all week to everyone who came into the store.

The Fifth Box

"Be with me when I die," Rosa had told him only two days earlier. From eleven at night until four in the morning he slept in brief spells beside her, waking every ten or twenty minutes to listen for her breathing. She had not spoken for twenty-four hours. Her eyes stayed open, wide and unblinking. Each time he woke, he heard the Cheyne-Stokes rhythm repeat itself: a long pause, a deep breath, three rapid shallow breaths, and a long pause. He looked past her to the bureau where the first of her boxes or assemblages rested. "A *real* one," Rosa said when she finished it ten years ago. "It's not 'Cornell fucks Schwitters' anymore." The steady rhythm changed into rapid panting. He waited for her last breath, and knew it when it came. With his thumbs he pulled the lids down over her green eyes.

Because it was early, he decided not to telephone anyone. Everybody knew that Rosa was dying. A week ago they had written her obituary together, and planned her cremation and memorial service: He would scatter her ashes in the meadow behind her studio. He sat looking at her white and whiter body. He needed to recognize and remember that Rosa was dead. Died. She was *dead*, a skeletal body, a wasted bald woman fifty-five years old forever.

Dawn shaded into the room. He had been told to call the visiting nurse. She would ascertain death, and then the undertaker would arrive with gurney and hearse. At seven he dialed the number, and the machine gave him a menu. As he recorded his message a dim voice interrupted him. "I'll be there in half an hour."

First there was something he needed to do. Two months ago, when she had been strong enough, Rosa had worked half an hour a day in her studio. Each late morning, he would build a fire in her Jøtul, and when the old shed was warm enough he would wrap Rosa in coats and blankets, help her walk, and leave her alone in a high chair at her workbench. She was making more boxes, tiny bizarre rooms furnished with bottle tops and broken glass and the world's debris. One afternoon, four weeks ago, when he looked in on Rosa after twenty minutes, she sat in the chair with her head on the bench. There would be no more boxes.

This morning he left her bedside, walked in cool dawn to open the shed, and turned on the glaring light that Rosa had worked by. Here was her bench with its tubes of glue and paint, fragments of an eggshell, and a goldfinch's feather. Against the wall were cubbyholes: a fishhook and pieces of yarn and a matchbook and rice and buttons and a toothpick and seashells and a thimble and pebbles.

On a long table across the room stood four finished boxes. There would be the posthumous show. On her workbench stood the fifth, unfinished box, with wallpaper striped on a wall, a wad of chewed gum, a seedpod, and a bird's egg among pencil marks where other objects would have gone. On the workbench, beside the box, he found an agate that looked like a glass eye, a battered doll, and the skull of a mouse. Rosa had spoken of the new box six weeks ago, her pale face luminous. "You can't look at it now. Too far to go."

Now he looked. Although his hands trembled, he would do what Rosa had asked him to do. He lifted the hatchet, with which she had chopped wood to fit the narrow stove, and struck the fifth box and split it and split the splittings. Then he howled in a rage that woke the dog at the farm next door, who howled and set other dogs howling. He took the ax to Rosa's bench and cut deep wedges into it, the top too thick to split, smashed the tubes of paint and glue, chopped off a table leg, shattered the cubbyholes along the wall, and with the blunt head of the ax cracked the enameled iron of her stove.

He lapsed on the scrappy floor. The dog howled once more and fell silent.

New England Primer

In 1937, Depression times, my mother left my father and me. I was seven years old, and she ran away with the town lawyer, my father's friend J. B. Burton. My father was Scytheville's doctor. While my father was in his office one morning, my mother packed a suitcase, left a letter, and walked to J. B. Burton's house. When I came back from school, my mother was absent and my father stood silent in the kitchen. "Your mother won't be with us," he said in a cracked voice. I didn't dare ask him why.

It was December, the kitchen range hot as he fried eggs for our supper. I watched him burn a letter in the firebox. When we sat at the kitchen table he broke his yolks and pushed his eggs around but did not eat them. "Your mother won't live with us anymore," he said. I burst into tears and clung to him.

"Minerva is leaving town with Mr. Burton," he told me. I was bewildered as well as bereft. I had never heard of a mother who left her family. I asked him why and he only held me tighter. Anguish and rage began that almost governed my life.

I don't know how or why the love affair happened. My parents did not quarrel in my presence, and I saw them kiss and hug. His office occupied the front room of our house, so that he was home most of the time, but he kept busy. He remained in his office mornings, with appointments, and in afternoons he drove the Model A to visit old people without automobiles. Weeknights he was exhausted, and often went to bed early while my mother read magazines: *Collier's, Life, The Saturday Evening Post.* Only on Sundays were my parents together, if there were no medical emergencies. She must have been lonely, and J. B. Burton could have courted her in the afternoon when I was in school and my father on his house calls.

After she left, he spoke of her only when he had to. People didn't bring the subject up. I found a neighbor setting a loaf of bread on our porch. She did not meet my eyes but said, "Billy." A pot of beans also turned up. The most anyone said to my father was "I'm sorry," treating my mother's flight like a death in the family.

At school a boy teased me. "Where'd your mother go, Billy?" Most of us were too young to know what men and women did. Our teacher flushed red. "That will be enough, Tom!" No one said anything again. For weeks my friends avoided playing with me. When they returned, I was aware of a blank place in our acquaintance.

My mother, as I remember her from early childhood, was slim and vivacious with large brown eyes, bobbed black hair, and red, red lipstick. She moved quickly as she cooked and cleaned house, then sometimes sat staring for an hour smoking cigarettes. Often she held me in her lap. Some occasions remained tender in my early memory, therefore corroded by what happened. When I was five, a small circus came to Blue River, ten miles away. My father dropped my mother and me off outside the tent on a Saturday afternoon, then picked us up after he had made his house calls. I remember the heightening buzz of voices, crowds jostling, the animal smells. We sat on pine benches watching high-wire acts and clowns, a droopy lion and its droopier tamer.

My mother wrapped an arm around me; she called me "Billy, Billy"; we held hands. She bought me a box of Cracker Jack.

My father, Henry Francis Root — "Doctor Frank" — was courteous, dependable, devoted to his duties, and decent without being unctuous. He had the nervous habit of cracking his knuckles, which came to irritate me. He was a *good* man, and above all he was disinterested; he was too disinterested. When my mother and J. B. Burton prepared to leave town, a week after she left us, Burton came to my father's office with a dislocated finger. I remember: We were having supper when there was a knock on the door. When I opened it, J. B. Burton stood there with one hand holding the other. "Your father?" he said, not looking me in the eye.

My father had followed me to the door. Burton showed him the askew, swollen finger. My father snapped it straight without speaking. Burton winced but made not a sound.

"Billy," said my father, "get me that roll of adhesive tape on the table next to my desk."

I brought it in. I could not look at J. B. Burton, and my father concentrated only on the finger. He could tape one digit to another without conversation. My father scissored and taped impassively, behaving as a doctor was supposed to behave. Finished, he pointed to the door. When Burton left, he did not have the temerity to thank my father.

When Burton and my mother drove away from Scytheville she did not say goodbye. From her journey west she sent me postcards telling me that she loved me and missed me. There were postmarks from Albany and Buffalo. A birthday present arrived from Chicago. Then there was a postcard from Reno, Nevada, and two months later my father told me that my mother had divorced him and married the man she was with. He would not say "J. B. Burton."

At first his sorrow and shock were visible only in silence and a tremor in his hands. I wept when I went to bed, as quietly as I could, imitating his reserve. One night I woke from sleep to hear him weeping also. He continued his daily routine, more slowly, energy depleted at thirty-seven. He lost weight. In the evenings he helped me with my homework, and on Saturdays took me in the car when he visited patients. He showed me cellarholes and abandoned smithies, the ruins of a New Hampshire that had been prosperous until the Civil War. Mornings my father saw that I was dressed and made me breakfast. Neighbor women took turns taking care of me after school, but such arrangements could not go on forever. My father looked for a housekeeper who would clean house, stay with me when I came home from school, and cook supper.

Even in the Depression, Scytheville was relatively prosperous. Not every small town had its own doctor. The mill laid off some hands—farmers sharpened their old scythes thin as oak leaves rather than buying new ones—but many citizens had jobs, and Scytheville Academy kept going, with day students and a few boarders. Like many American towns, Scytheville paired itself with a poorer cousin. The shack people lived in Liberty, three miles away. If a Scytheville housewife's arthritis precluded wash-ing and cooking, she went to Liberty for household help.

At that time, families were known to be either good or bad. There were good, impoverished families in Liberty (as there were in Scytheville) who had no money but ate from big gardens, canned, boiled maple sap for sweet, kept a pig, cut down trees for heat, and shot a deer every November. They lived in a plenty of food and warmth. The bad people in Liberty survived on hard cider with intervals of seasonal work.

Thus, when my father needed a housekeeper, he looked to Liberty. First he hired Mrs. Boswell, a widow who spent the day listening to radio soap operas, fifteen minutes each: *Ma Perkins, Just Plain Bill,* and *Mary Noble, Backstage Wife.* She talked as if the plots and the people were real: "That Lorenzo! He ought to get a job like anyone else." "I wonder how old Ma is. She sounds *old.*" After school I partook of her habit, and late in the afternoon we listened together to a cowboy singer. Mrs. Boswell seldom cleaned or tidied, and dust piled on top of clutter. My father had to let her go.

To replace Mrs. Boswell, he found Ruby Moody, also from Liberty, who turned fourteen in 1938 and dropped out of school to earn money for her family. When Ruby arrived she was an awk-ward schoolgirl, tall, with broad shoulders, who never smiled. My father introduced me in his courtly fashion, and Ruby looked straight into me. "What do I do with him?"

If she was shy, she covered it up by grudging everything. She was certainly gruff with me. Her lower lip stuck out as if it ex-pressed petulance. I liked it that she was a girl — but I was scared of her. I sought her favor. At first her cooking was primitive: overcooked vegetables, chicken, boiled potatoes, more lard than seemed possible. My father complimented her. She needed compliments. He found her a Fannie Farmer cookbook. After a while she looked more comfortable, and it pleased me to come home to her after school. "What did you do today?" she said, maybe as she made biscuits.

"Nothing," I said. "Can you play?"

"In a minute."

The summer I was eight, my father took me with him on his house calls, sometimes to remote places. Once he stopped the car on an old wood road up Biscuit Hill, nearly to Liberty, when our new Packard could go no further. Horses, or more likely oxen, had hauled timber here, over great granite lumps that would smash a crankcase. We walked keeping to the ruts. My father carried his black bag and I walked beside him, avoiding poison ivy and thorny blackberry bushes. "Where are we going?" I said.

"To Belle's shack," he said. "You remember Belle?"

I didn't know her last name but I knew who Belle was. Everybody did. The woods were full of old men who lived alone, nature's bachelors; Belle was the only woman.

She was eighty years old. She did not live quite alone because she had a sixty-year-old son named Gospel, who was feeble-minded and lived mostly in the woods. I'd never seen him. I asked my father about Belle and Gospel. "Well, they say she was born on a farm where her shack is, ran off in a family way when she was nineteen, and came back with Gospel twenty years later. She's got a dug well, a pump, and an outhouse. She sends me a penny postcard when she wants me to look in on her. It's her hips. Aspirin's the only thing."

"What about Gospel's father?" I asked, thinking, of course, of my missing mother.

"Nobody knows about the father."

By this time I knew just enough not to ask another question.

We passed dense birches. Saplings rose beside the fallen birches. We passed a cellarhole that my father called the Buzzle place. We walked past stone walls among the birches, woods that had once been pasture, and through a grown-over apple orchard and a hemlock forest. The trees stopped as we entered a clearing, where we saw a great patch of hollyhocks in front of Belle's shack. An old dog howled once when he saw us, then dragged himself upright and wagged his tail. My father scratched him behind the ears.

Belle's place was unpainted boards nailed upright with deer-skin stapled onto them. "She made her shack with what was left of the farmhouse. She must have pulled that captain's chair out of the old place."

"Doctor Frank," Belle said. She took her small glasses off, to see me better, and I saw deep red marks high at the sides of her nose where the glasses pinched. She wore a man's shoes without laces, and she limped.

Belle waved us into her room-house and took a black pot off the single chair. She filled a kettle, dipping the water out of a pail, and opened the drafts on her rusty woodstove. A shape embossed on the oven door looked like a peacock's tail. Her stomach pushed into the stove, leaving her apron black. She found a jar of Nescafé. "All you have to do is pour hot water over it," she said.

While Belle and my father talked about her miseries, I looked around the shack. I saw a cigar box of eyeglasses like the ones she was wearing. Why did she keep a whole box? In other boxes, nailed to a two-by-four, I saw buttons, beads, knitting needles, a crochet hook . . . Against the wall I saw shelves of canning: beans, peas, shelled corn, one pint of tomatoes, honey in combs. I saw a bugle hanging from a nail. A small forest of canes grew out of a milk can.

My father measured out pills for Belle, probably samples from Bayer. "We used to get aspirin from Germany," said my father.

"New war started yet?" said Belle. "We in it?"

He shook his head. "Not yet," he said.

She looked at me. "I remember the soldier boys come back from the Civil War," she said. "Do you see my bugle?"

I knew about the Civil War; my father read books about it. His grandfather fought through Tennessee, the 11th New Hampshire Infantry; we had a blue cap he'd worn.

"That's a Union bugle, brought back by a man walked home from Virginia."

The door darkened and the figure of a big man filled it, tall with a huge belly. He was carrying small birch logs toward the woodstove. When his eyes adjusted from outdoors, he saw my father and me. He dropped the wood and ran out the door into the woods.

"Gospel's a good boy," said Belle, "even if he's not right." I peeked out the door to see if he was lurking somewhere. Belle said, "Gospel and that bugle come from the same place." She made a sound like a giggle. She looked at my father, no longer addressing me. "The whited sepulcher brought it back from the war. When I showed, he fired me."

"Well," said my father, getting up from the chair, stretching, his black bag in his hand, "you've done right by yourself and Gospel. Why did you call him Gospel?"

"When I came back everything was tumbled down, even the mill. I called him Gospel because his father was a whited sepulcher."

Belle turned to me. "It's like that old primer," she said. From the jumble of her shack she picked up a small square book. "*The New England Primer*," she said as she handed it to me. I saw mottled pages with old printing and woodcuts stained with age. "My mother taught me my ABCs from that book," she said.

Then she looked at my father, smiling without teeth. "In Adam's fall," she said, "we sinnèd all."

Ruby slept upstairs in the spare room and returned to Liberty every other weekend, taking her salary with her. My father paid her five dollars a week plus room and board. Ruby was changing, no longer gruff—disarmed, I think, by my father's courtliness. We were both taken with her.

Along with cleaning house and washing and ironing and cooking, Ruby's job was me. I loved coming home from school. By the year I turned nine, and the war started in Europe, I was in love with her. She agreed to wait and marry me when I was old enough. We played together at first, tossing a tennis ball back and forth, taking our turns on a swing that hung from a stout branch of maple. We pushed each other to get started, then pumped and soared. I liked touching her buttocks. We walked together upstream past the scythe mill and climbed on stones that had supported other mills. She had heard about Belle but not about Gospel.

She never spoke of my mother. I woke up angry in the night and soothed myself thinking of Ruby.

Once when she was pushing me on the swing, I fell onto the roots of a tree.

"Billy!" said Ruby. "Are you all right? I'll get your father. You poor dear!"

When I stood and shook myself and convinced her that I was all right, she took me inside to the sofa and rubbed me where it hurt. I didn't want her to stop.

"Once my father fell and broke his arm," she said. "He was drunk," she said. I heard her turn angry. "He hits my mother."

It was horrid to know that Ruby came from such a house, such a family, but I knew Liberty's reputation.

My father worried that I played too little with boys my own age, and encouraged visits from my fourth-grade friends. There were only twelve scholars in our red one-room school. Maybe my father asked Ruby not to play with me so much. When I wanted to toss a ball with her, usually she had too much to do. Or maybe she just grew older. By sixteen she had lost her childishness, leaving me a little lonesome—though sometimes she still let me push her on the swing.

That spring Otto Buzzard, older brother of my schoolmate Tom, found reasons to drop by the house. He knocked at the door to the kitchen where Ruby baked and cooked. His blond hair straggled under an Esso cap. He said, "Corn's up," or "What're you doing?" or "Looks like snow." Half the time his mouth slacked open as he stared at Ruby in her long housedress. She scuttled about, aware of Otto's attentions. At ten I knew enough to be jealous of him.

My father decided that Ruby ought to continue her education. She could read and write, but she hadn't read much of anything. My father wanted to keep her from being a Liberty Moody, or a Mrs. Otto Buzzard of Scytheville. Near us lived a married woman who had been a teacher, and my father hired her to tutor Ruby in grammar, geography, reading, math, and general science. Algebra was hard. Ruby took to her studies reluctantly, but she wanted to please my father. When Otto dropped by she put him off: No, she could not go out walking with him. She had homework. Otto's visits dwindled, and he joined the army three months after Pearl Harbor.

Every evening, my father and Ruby and I sat together around the parlor woodstove. I did homework or read stories about aviators in the Great War while another war started. My father read medical journals and history books. You could tell he was really taken with a book when he didn't crack his knuckles. I lifted my eyes from my schoolbook to watch Ruby's face as she worked at her studies or looked into my father's history books, practicing her reading. At seventeen or eighteen she started to be beautiful, without knowing it. Her young face with its strong features frowned down on her schoolwork, her lower lip protruding only a little. She wasn't always good-natured. One night my father cracked his knuckles more than ever and kept quoting phrases from the book he was reading. "The battle of Bennington," he might say, not realizing that he was speaking out loud. Ruby threw her algebra book on the floor and slammed the door of her room upstairs.

With her new schoolwork, Ruby walked less frequently now to Liberty. Once a month she hiked there on a Sunday, taking her dollars. One night, my father and I were eating a cold Sunday supper when Ruby came in the back door. We both cried out. Her eyes were black and her lip split, blood on her chin. She wept as we looked at her. My father dampened a washcloth and cleaned off the blood, examining her mouth and her eyes. "I ain't never going back there," she said.

"I'm not ever going back," my father corrected her. "Your father?"

Ruby nodded. "My father. While my mother watched and my brothers. He said book learning wasn't for women."

"You can stay here. Until you go to college."

"I'm happy here," she said, looking frightened.

Ruby was admitted, by examination, to the senior year at Scytheville Academy. She did well enough to be accepted by the normal school at Keene in 1943. She was nineteen, and thought about teaching kindergarten. My father paid her tuition, room and board, which didn't add up to much. To visit us weekends, she took a train into Boston's North Station and another out to Blue River. My father met her at the depot, 12:38 P.M. on Saturday. She came every weekend, cooking and studying, and went back Sunday night. Something was changing in her. She had a life away from us. She talked about sociology, or the girl she worked with in a chemistry lab. She showed us B+ papers, and my father praised

her. Weekdays were lonesome for us; we made do. Sometimes
Mrs. Ewell came over.

One day Bert Bottoms, the RFD man, burst into my father's office hours to cry out that Belle was hurt. "Bad hurt, up to her
shack." When she had not emptied her mailbox for days — fliers,
I suppose — Bert walked in and found her lying supine in her
cabin, half out of her mind. Gospel ran away when he saw Bert.
My father called the Blue River ambulance, met it at the wood
road, and showed the way. Belle raved, she wouldn't leave
Gospel, but the men lifted her onto the stretcher and took her to
the hospital at Blue River. She had broken a hip.

She fretted about Gospel until she died, eighty-six years old.
The town buried her. I wondered what happened to the Civil War
bugle. By now I knew what she meant by whited sepulcher. I
wondered if anybody ever found the little square book.

My father and Bert and others looked for Gospel. They only
glimpsed him as he ran to hide. Each week, Bert left two loaves of
bread and a pound of rat cheese for him, wrapped in tinfoil, tied
in a bundle against raccoons and squirrels. When Bert came back
each time, last week's food was gone.

When I saw my father and Ruby kissing in the kitchen — they
thought I was upstairs — I was horrified. My father was forty-four
years old and Ruby was twenty! My father was plump and bald-
ing. He plodded; Ruby bounced when she walked. I was furious
and hated what they felt. By now I knew what desire was because
I woke with it every morning. Maybe her difficult early life made
her seem older than other twenty-year-old girls. Still, Ruby's

youthful beauty is clear in my memory. I can find only one picture, taken when she was nineteen standing beside me at thirteen. She smiles and leans my way, light behind her so that I can see the curve of her leg through her dress. Her hair is shaggy as it tilts toward me. The lower lip looks sensual, instead of seeming to pout.

One Sunday they took me aside and told me: When Ruby finished her degree, she and my father would marry.

"We're happy," my father said. "It must be strange for you."

"I'm thinking about starting a nursery school in Blue River," said Ruby, suddenly older and separate. "It's getting big enough. It's prosperous." I remembered when Ruby would not have used a word like "prosperous." I suppose she thought of a private nursery school.

Grudgingly I came to accept their marriage, though I know I withdrew from my happy father. He withdrew a little from me, too. I was jealous of both of them but came to understand that it was good that Ruby would remain in my life. When it was my turn to attend college I would come home to Ruby and my father together. And I could come home to Miriam, an Academy student I was sweet on.

At birthdays and Christmases I received my mother's packages, now from California, with notes signed, "Your loving Mother." My father had a Christmas card signed by Minerva but not by J.B. Naturally his hurt had diminished. Then, early in 1945, on a Thursday, I found in the day's mail a thick letter addressed to my father in my mother's handwriting. When I handed it to him he looked troubled and took it with him into his office, closing the door. An hour later he emerged—pale, shaking, eyes red—to Mrs. Ewell's supper. I asked him what was wrong. I knew it was my mother's letter. He blew his nose on the cloth handkerchief he carried in his jacket pocket. "I can't say anything now."

The next day he canceled office hours and drove away by himself. When he came back for supper he was silent. I was frightened. He touched my arm. He said, "I'm sorry, Billy," and resumed his silence. Saturday, before he drove to pick up Ruby at Blue River, he told me that he and Ruby would take a ride before they came home. I knew that they would talk, and that they would talk because of my mother's letter. When they returned Ruby climbed quickly to her room. My father asked me into his office.

"I telegraphed money to California. To your mother. She's coming back."

I could not believe what I heard. "*Ruby* . . ." I said.

"I telegraphed your mother money for the train. She has nothing and nobody. She's sick."

"I don't want her back!"

"She's sick. Very sick. She's penniless. I have to take her back." I saw my father start to weep, and I knew he was not weeping for my mother. "Her husband"—my father still wouldn't say the name—"shot himself two months ago. Bankrupt. Minerva has no place to go. Ruby knows that I have to take her in. Ruby will keep on at college and still come here weekends. Minerva will die, but it might take a long time. I told Ruby that she was free." I ran upstairs to my room in a rage against both my mother and father.

· · ·

My father took me with him to pick up my mother at the Blue River depot. I didn't know the frail frowning woman with one suitcase who gazed at us. Her illness exaggerated her age, and she was wobbly when she walked. My father said, "Minerva," and picked up her bag.

"Thank you," she said. Her forehead was creased, her mouth curved down. "You look better than me. The trains are worse than ever." She looked at me. "You're big now, Billy," she said. "You're too big for that coat. I knew you'd take me back, though I don't know why you should." When she hugged me I felt cold coming from her bones. Maybe it was my bones the cold came from.

On the drive back she spoke sparely. "It's as grimy here as ever," she said. "In California the sun shines."

Her fingers shook when she lit a cigarette. My heart wanted to stop itself. I loathed this bony whiner.

That night my father cracked his knuckles incessantly. He cracked them incessantly every night. "Stop that," my mother snapped. He kept on. Every night I left them in the dining room or parlor and went to my room.

Ruby returned four weekends in a row and slept on the sofa because the spare room was Minerva's, medicine smells and sour sickbed linen. One Sunday morning, Minerva's voice rose into a tirade at Ruby. Who did she think she *was*, her nose in a book when Mrs. Ewell needed help in the kitchen? My father shouted, "Shut up, Minerva!" I had never heard him use such words.

That afternoon, Ruby and I slipped out of the house to take a walk like our old walks. When I spoke bitterly about my mother, Ruby did not hush me. On the fourth weekend my father did his

Saturday rounds and met Ruby's train. While he was gone my mother laughed without stopping, an eerie sound. When my father brought Ruby home, laughter turned into uncontrolled weeping. I did not know it, but the intermittent crying and laughing were symptoms of her disease, like her slurred speech. She had ALS, which people called Lou Gehrig's disease.

For Ruby, her visits became intolerable. My father said that she needn't come home all the time. The next weekend, without having warned us, she did not step down from the train. Nor the next weekend nor the next. My father wrote her daily at her Keene address. After two weeks, his letters began to return, and a form arrived at the house, addressed to Ruby, that my father opened and read. The dean of women at the normal school wrote that because of Miss Moody's absence from classes, and because Miss Moody had left her Keene address, the dean was forced to conclude that Miss Moody was no longer a student. Unless she received a satisfactory explanation . . .

My father and I left my mother with Mrs. Ewell. We drove to Keene. Her landlady told us that Ruby had packed her suitcases and moved out three weeks ago, that she had stopped going to classes earlier. A young man in a Model A had driven her away. We headed back to Scytheville in a double silence of anxiety and melancholy. "Where could she go?" I said.

"To Liberty," said my father, and turned away from our Scytheville road. When we parked by the Moody shack its door swung open and the left side of the porch drooped. The nearest neighbor told us that the Moodys had left town and good riddance. No, they didn't know about the daughter, just the mister and missus. The twins had moved out a long time ago. One store in Liberty was open, but the owner knew nothing except that old Moody owed him eighteen dollars.

V-E Day. V-J Day.

I overheard my father on the telephone seeking information from the New Hampshire, and later the Massachusetts, State Police. No, he told them, he could not file a missing persons report. He hired a detective who was unable to trace her.

My mother lay in bed and rose holding on to furniture when she had to use the upstairs bathroom my father had installed for her. Slobbering, she scolded Mrs. Ewell. My quiet father yelled at my mother, and she yelled back or went into one of her weeping jags. I hated my house. As she became frailer and more depressed, sometimes she spent days without speaking. She had to stay in bed all day. Bedpans. The visiting nurse helped, but Mrs. Ewell was running out of strength. My father hired a nurse's helper who drove from Blue Hill. Some days my mother thanked my father over and over. Once she patted me on the hand and said, "Billy, Billy." I pulled my hand away.

By the time I entered my last year at Scytheville Academy, I had lost all interest in stone walls and cellarholes. They were the vacancy and rottenness of this place. I came home from the Academy as late as I could, often not until suppertime. I smoked cigarettes in the woods with other Academy criminals. At home I didn't answer when spoken to. If my father spoke to me sternly, I left the house, which was forbidden. My father was losing me as he had lost everything else.

After another year, with my mother sinking into paralysis, I went to Boston University, planning to go on to business school.

I would be rich and travel the world and never return to Scytheville.

My mother died the next year. After the funeral I saw her buried in the family plot, and hurried back to Boston. I accelerated my studies, for early admission to Harvard Business School, and came home little. My father moved with a ponderous slowness, although he was only fifty. Mrs. Ewell, an old woman, could just keep my father's house in order. He took dinner at the Scytheville Inn, sitting alone night after night until Mason Thirlwell joined him, an old neighbor and a widower. After dinner they played checkers.

I let my courses absorb me. I felt superior to my father, with a young man's arrogance, because his exaggerated goodness had wasted his life. I asked him to call me William, and corrected him if he forgot. My father took long naps on Sunday afternoons, although his working week was less strenuous. Old people without cars had died off; the young drove to Blue River to see their internists.

I visited Scytheville a few times a year. One Sunday afternoon in 1951, the summer before I went to Harvard, I paid a call on my old girlfriend Miriam, then took my father's 1947 Ford and drove around the countryside, up dirt roads and down, past cellarholes where I had waited in the car as my father visited cantankerous patients. He had told me that Gospel's food now went untouched. When I found myself on the outskirts of Liberty, on impulse I turned into town, to the street where Ruby had grown up. To my surprise the house was standing, the porch leveled by stacked concrete blocks. A crone rocked on the porch. Parking, I hesitated, then walked up the creaking stairs. Maybe this woman was the remains of Ruby's mother. "Are you Mrs. Moody?" I asked.

"Who be you?" she said from her toothless mouth.

"I used to know . . . the Moodys," I said. I was afraid to ask.

"Well I don't know ye . . . He's been dead a long time ago."

A girl of about three clattered out on the porch through the torn screen door, and I saw in the shadow behind her a tall woman's figure.

Ruby's hand lifted to cover her mouth, and I had time to see that her lower lip no longer pouted forward. "Billy," she said. I didn't mind "Billy" from Ruby. "You've grown up." She dropped her hand; some front teeth were missing. Much of Liberty was toothless by thirty-five. Her hair straggled; she was ragged in pants and a worn checked shirt. A cigarette poked out of her mouth, and she did not smile. I could begin to see her mother in Ruby.

"I didn't want to tell you, your father, that I was back. It's only two months."

"Where have you been?" I said. "We looked for you."

Ruby shrugged. "I kept myself away. I didn't want to fool myself. I heard your mother died." She held the girl by both shoulders. "This is my daughter," she said, "Dorothy. I wait on table down to the Liberty Tavern. This is where me and Dorothy belong. Don't tell your father I'm here."

"He'll find out," I said.

Ruby and her daughter backed into the dark hallway. "I had her by myself," she said as she disappeared.

Driving back toward Scytheville, I parked the car to walk by the stream where Ruby and I had walked among the ghost mills. I stayed until late, angry at both my parents, at Ruby, at the place where I was born. In two days I would return to Boston, leaving my father — and now leaving Ruby, who had turned back into a Liberty Moody. I couldn't bear to tell my father, who was already so broken. It would not bother him that she had a child, but it would destroy him that she had become a Moody again.

My father was a letter writer, not fond of the telephone. Every Wednesday in Boston, across the Charles from the rest of Harvard, I received a handwritten letter of some length, his Sunday morning's work. His language was formal in its constructions, but it allowed the show of affection. I wrote him back, not so well nor so often. In my mind I continued to see Ruby and her daughter, Ruby with her hand over her mouth, enjoining me not to tell my father.

The summer of 1953, I spent two weeks in Scytheville seeing school friends, including my girlfriend Miriam who was married, and visiting my father who worked still fewer hours. One afternoon he and I drove and walked, mostly in silence, on the dirt roads lined by stone walls. Maybe this would be the last time. I'd come back to say goodbye to everything. Businesses were recruiting and I had already interviewed for jobs in Chicago, Los Angeles, even London. As we walked my father puffed, although he had lost weight.

Once, while my father had office hours, I drove to Liberty where I did and did not want to see Ruby. I watched her hanging laundry in her back yard, smoking and wearing shorts on a hot August day, with her five-year-old daughter handing her wet wash. She was another impoverished young mother of Liberty. I paused on the road to watch, and when she turned to look in my direction, I drove on.

With my father and Mason Thirlwell I ate at the Scytheville Inn, and kibitzed while they played checkers. My father's life was over at fifty-three. Why had no one told him that Ruby had come back? The town's manners were silence and reticence.

Not long after I went back to Boston a letter arrived from my father. In calm tones, expressing no dread or anxiety, he told me that he had cancer of the colon. I remembered how tired he had seemed, and that he had lost weight. He had observed blood in his stool, and at Blue Hill Hospital a barium enema revealed a mass high in his colon. It would be malignant, he told me, but it was small, and his chances were good that the cancer would not return. He was to be operated on the next day. I was on no account to leave my studies but to remain in Boston and wait for word from Mason Thirlwell. He would stay in the hospital about a week.

The next morning, I borrowed a roommate's car and drove to Blue Hill. When I arrived my father was in recovery. The surgeon confirmed that the tumor was malignant, but small and within the walls of the colon.

I was permitted to enter the recovery room, where nurses scuttled among patients just returned from surgery. My father was sedated, in pain, but his usual calmness showed through: Now it was useful that my father was tolerant of disaster. I went into town for lunch and returned to see him in intensive care. The next day I sat beside his bed, and we could talk easily when he first had morphine, but quickly he became sleepy. I stayed with him two days, then returned to my case studies and left Mason Thirlwell to visit him. When he returned home, weak, neighbors would help, and Mason, and a visiting nurse.

But I worried for him. Mason was a good friend, but I could not see him as a caretaker. Then I thought of an improbable solution, for my father's comfort and my own. When Scytheville needed help, it went to Liberty. The next weekend — my father due home on Monday — I borrowed the car again and drove not to Blue Hill or Scytheville but to Liberty. Ruby was in her nightgown at noon, fixing lunch for Dorothy. She looked frightened to see me; I must have looked anxious. She asked, "Your father?"

I told her about the cancer and that she must come back to the house where she had lived from fourteen to twenty. My father would need her. She shook her head. "I have Dorothy," she said.

"You loved my father," I said. "You still do. He never stopped loving you. Come back with Dorothy and move in. Take care of him when he comes home from the hospital." She kept shaking her head. "He needs you. When he's better, you can go back to Liberty if you want."

By the time Dorothy came in from play, Ruby had packed their things into paper bags. She gave her daughter lunch and took her aside to say that they were going to Scytheville to care for a sick man she used to know. Dorothy was a solemn child. She nodded without speaking. Ruby worried about how she looked; she worried about her clothes. In the Kresge's at Blue River I bought new clothes for Ruby and Dorothy. Ruby, in her distraction, seemed to pick her new things almost at random. She was typically frugal. Dorothy and she changed into new clothes in a changing room, and left behind the garments they had been wearing.

When we drove toward Scytheville Ruby continued to fret: "Maybe I'm doing the wrong thing again. I shouldn't have let your mother drive me out."

She went pale as we approached town. Dorothy was silent, as if caught in a dream. I helped them carry their few things into the house Ruby knew so well, then drove with her to the hospital. We left Dorothy with Mason Thirlwell, clearly uncomfortable with a little girl. Alone with my father, I told him what I had done: I had brought Ruby back from Liberty, with a daughter just turned five, and I had settled her in our house to take care of him while he was weak. He wept and shook his head. I did not know what he was thinking, but I saw that part of him was both incredulous and overjoyed. He thanked me and asked me if I had brought Ruby to the hospital. I led her from the waiting room to his bedside where they gazed at each other. "Ruby," said my father.

"Will you be all right?" said Ruby. "Is it all right if I take care of you?" There were no tears in her eyes among the beginning wrinkles. "I never finished normal school."

"Thank heaven for Billy," said my father. "You . . ." He wanted to tell her that he wished she had come back sooner.

"You know about Dorothy? Billy told you."

He was getting tired and showed it. He took Ruby's hand. I tried to see the changed Ruby through my father's eyes: her teeth, her new wrinkles.

After I returned to school, Mason drove my father home to Ruby's care. I telephoned every day. In a week, my father was writing me letters again. Ruby added postscripts. Most weekends I visited them. Ruby cooked in the kitchen of her girlhood, tall and reserved and handsome at thirty. She had changed in a decade. She no longer bounced when she walked. Her mouth curved down, and looked dour, but she stopped smoking. Gradually my father gained strength and took up his small practice again. After six weeks Ruby no longer occupied the spare room. They were married a month later in a judge's chambers in Blue River.

After graduation, I returned for a week to Scytheville before taking a good job in Salt Lake City. Dorothy was finishing the year in the multigrade school, and Ruby had a new bridge that looked natural. My father at fifty-four was more sprightly than he had been since 1945. Rarely did he crack his knuckles. On this visit I walked with both of them in the countryside among the ruins again. Utah began to seem far away. My father told me that deer hunters had found Gospel's skeleton in the ruins of Belle's camp.

Back in Boston, I telegraphed my regrets to Utah and looked for work in the Northeast. Thus I settled in Portland, Maine, and married a Radcliffe student I had met in Cambridge. Dorothy grew tall like her mother and became a joy of my father's late middle age. He told her all the stories. When my marriage fell apart, I was ready to move from Portland to Boston, with a job similar to my old one. I liked to visit Scytheville, where Ruby and my father lived quietly and with clear affection. Dorothy was a lower-middler at the Academy, and wanted to go to Smith or Mount Holyoke. Life seemed almost reparable. Then I remembered my mother's leaving and returning, Ruby's exile, my father alone, my divorce. In Adam's fall We sinnèd all.

A year after I moved to Boston, nine years after Ruby's return, she telephoned me at the office midweek to tell me that my father had had a heart attack. I notified my staff and drove to Blue Hill on the new highway. My father was in intensive care again, and switched to the cardiac unit a day later. When Ruby left the room to have lunch, he told me from his long experience that he probably didn't have more than a year or two.

He died nineteen months later, Ruby and Dorothy beside him. We buried him next to Minerva, his last disinterested request, with a place for Ruby on his other side.

I go to Scytheville often, to see Ruby and Dorothy. We take walks where Ruby and I rambled so many years before. The old people have died off. Only Ruby and I can discern, among the stones and the new growth, the remains of the old farms and cellarholes. For Dorothy, now teaching at the Academy, we are archeologists at the site of Troy. Summer cottages and retirement communities are beginning to take over, filled with people who love the countryside but don't know its history. Senior citizens from the suburbs of Boston and Toledo have founded a Scytheville-Liberty Historical Association and a community center. Grandchildren of the shack people now mow the lawns and plow the snow.

Driving up Biscuit Hill one day with Ruby and Dorothy, I pulled into an unwooded bite beside newly bulldozed forest. Developers were advertising a new retirement community. The ruts looked like Belle's wood road, and the three of us walked on flattened sand beside pushed-over birches and hemlocks. Huge yellow engines squatted in the weekend silence. Clearing had just begun, and we walked to its far edge easily, to look into dense woods that would become lawns — as, two hundred years earlier, virgin forest had yielded acre by acre to pasture and hayfield. One hollyhock raised a skinny stem. I saw a heap of boards soon to be dozed into a hollow and covered with dirt. I kicked at the leaves, my heart pounding, and nudged into sight a pair of old-fashioned eyeglasses. When I squeezed them onto my nose, the landscape brightened and enlarged. Ruby tried them on, and then Dorothy.

Grateful acknowledgment is made to the publishers of earlier versions of these stories: *Antaeus* ("Argument and Persuasion"), *The Atlantic Monthly* ("From Willow Temple" and "New England Primer"), *Boulevard* ("Lake Paradise"), *The Georgia Review* ("The First Woman," under the title "The World Is a Bed"), *The New Yorker* ("Christmas Snow"), *The Ohio Review* ("The Figure of the Woods," "The Ideal Bakery," and "The Accident"), *The Ontario Review* ("The Fifth Box"), and *The Yale Review* ("Roast Suckling Pig").

"From Willow Temple" was reprinted in *The Best American Short Stories 1997*.

The Ideal Bakery (North Point Press, 1987) included "Argument and Persuasion," "The First Woman," "Christmas Snow," "The Figure of the Woods," and "The Ideal Bakery."